Steps To Freedom
Reshad Feild

Steps To Freedom

Discourses on the Alchemy of the Heart

Reshad Feild

Threshold Books
Putney, Vermont
1983

Threshold Books is committed to publishing books of spiritual significance with high literary quality. All Threshold books have sewn bindings, and are printed on acid-free paper.

We will be happy to send you a catalog.
Threshold Books, RD 3, Box 1350, Putney, Vermont 05346

Library of Congress Catalog Card Number 83-050115
ISBN 0-939660-04-0

The Library of Congress has cataloged the first printing of this title as follows:

Feild, Reshad.
   Steps to freedom : discourses on the alchemy of the heart /
Reshad Feild. - Putney, Vt. : Threshold Books, 1983.

   163 p. ; 21 cm.
   ISBN 0-939660-04-0 (pbk.) : $9.00

   1. Sufism.   I. Title.
BP189.6.F45   1983   297'.4-dc19   83-50115
                           AACR 2   MARC

I dedicate this book to the necessary transformation of this planet.

CONTENTS

From the Author   ix

Foreword   xi

Intention   1

Asking the Question   4

The Need for Real Change   11

Conscious Love   20

Remembrance, Meditation, Trust, and Service   26

Freedom   33

The Search for Identity   40

The Path of Return   43

The Need for Will   50

Decision   53

Developing Will   57

Attunement   64

Humility and the Action of Love   69

Types of Food   71

The Recognition of Truth   74

The Sole Purpose of Love Is Beauty   76

Conscious Suffering   81

Breath   89

Making Love   92

Desire   96

Breaking Through Separation   101

The Fixing of Gold in the Heart   104

Barriers to Transformation   106

Beginning the Work   109

Transformation of Energies   111

Being and Capacity   116

Pattern   121

Community   126

Brotherhood   131

Serving the Guest   135

Prayer   137

Die Before You Die   142

Lordship   144

The Path of the Mystic   146

The Symbolism of the Wedding Ceremony   150

The Limitations of the Mind   153

The Creation of a Soul   155

The Alchemy of the Heart   159

From the author:

I would ask the reader to be patient, since this is not a book in the normal sense of the word. The chapters are compiled from over one hundred typed transcripts of talks that I have given over the years. Thus, there are repetitions in different chapters which I have chosen to keep in the manuscript in order to preserve the spirit of the original.

Sometimes what lies behind the words is best understood if the chapters are read aloud in a group or when two or three people can find the time to sit down and mull over what has been said. Each chapter is complete in itself, and yet the book as a whole has a certain sequence. There are, as well, paragraphs which could serve for extended study.

I offer this book as a contribution to the new age into which we are inevitably moving, step by step, as the past is redeemed into the present moment, and the future is seen to be here —now!

Reshad Feild
Santa Cruz, California

Acknowledgments

First of all I would like to thank all those who have worked so hard to make this book possible over the years: Matt Shoemaker who spent night after night working in the basement (where he was sleeping at the time!). Kabir and Camille Helminski and Blair Tremoureux for their diligent appraisal of the work already done and their most helpful suggestions and further editing. George Witterschein for his detailed and thoughtful editing. Subhana Menis without whose kindness and thoughtfulness as my secretary this manuscript would never have been typed. And Penny Belknap who helped in so many ways.

Reshad Feild

FOREWORD

O nce upon a time, when the world was very young, there was harmony. There was one rhythm, one breath, the breath of unity. The world turned. Once upon a time. But once upon that time, that one-moment, a new rhythm evolved from the rhythm of harmony. A new breath was born. There came another sort of time upon the time of natural order. From the breath and rhythm of God there came the breath of man . . . once upon a time.

So there came about two rhythms, two breaths, and the tension created by the two brought about the two great Commandments: "Love the Lord thy God" and "Love thy neighbor as thyself." Then there could be harmony once again.

But mankind has never remembered, and so at certain times of history we are offered, once again, the chance to turn straight to our Lord, to take the path of Return. We are offered the chance when things seem to be at their worst, when order has failed and chaos rules, when mankind has forgotten to love, when God has been forgotten.

In essence we are one. It is easy to pay lip service to a concept, to see it in the mind as an idea, rather than to know it through the direct perception of the heart. We are one in essence, but we have to know this, and then we consciously carry all of mankind in our hearts. To say that we know of our essential unity and to ignore the suffering of mankind is to fail to obey the second of the two great commandments. To do good deeds for mankind and not to turn straight to God is to ignore the existence of the First Cause . . . two commandments, two great laws, night and day, heaven and earth, yin and yang, man and woman.

Hope—what is hope? So often it merely leads to its relative opposite. What is that but despair? Yet there is hope. There is real hope when men and women awake from their state of sleep to turn, little by little—to become real, conscious human beings, responsible for themselves and their families, responsible for their groups and society, responsible for their villages, their cities, and for the very land of which they are the custodians.

It is hard to hear hope or see hope. It is hard even to feel hope in a world that has lost all sense of reason, in a world which has come to rely only on form. Reliance on form finally brings about complete disillusionment, chaos, fear, grief, and even apathy, in the face of the beauty of God's creation.

Yet from the beginning there has always been the possibility of real hope. We could call it "objective hope." It is hope that has an object; and that object does not come about from blind superstition, nor from systems, nor from ritual, nor from magic. It comes about from and within real knowledge.

INTENTION *"Without right motive and right intention, we cannot fulfill our destiny in being born man and woman."*

Before anything is undertaken in life, it is wise to consider very deeply the nature and quality of our motive. If our motive is not pure, then whatever we set out to achieve is unlikely to bring about good results. It is true to say, "Whatsoever you sow, so shall you reap." It is a foolish man who sets out on a journey without first considering his motive, and without knowing a little about the results of setting an intention.

Almost everything we do in this world is unconscious and based on reactions from the conditioned mind, which is in a state of "sleep." The average man, sleepwalking his way through life, seldom if ever goes into the questions of motive and intention. He is tossed about by waves of fate, the control of which has already slipped from his hands. He does not know that he is asleep. The result of this sleep can lead him only into further sleep states. Not only does he not know the purpose of life, but he does not even care to question why he was born and what he is doing in this world at this time. He actually considers that he can "do" something. He thinks that he can think a thought, whereas in reality a thought thinks him. Until he awakens to serve the present moment, thought-forms influence his life. These thought-forms are materialized from the biosphere through human beings who do not realize that they are vehicles for the Divine Will and transformers of subtle energies. We each have a job to do, which is to be of service in this world. And then the law of the real world can be brought into ordered manifestation here and now.

Even if our motive is good, it is rare that we ever fulfill our original intention. The power of the original intention will diminish if it has been deviated by negative emotions or feelings, which get in the way of what we set out to do in the first place. Then there can be wastage of energy, and energy is surely needed to make any decision. Energy follows thought, and unless the thought is directed in a straight line, there is bound to be deviation of the energy as it spreads itself out along the lines of thought. Obviously, the end result achieved would be small indeed.

It does not matter what example we use, be it a journey to the office or to the market. How many times have we gone to the market to buy a certain type of food and come home having forgotten what we originally went for? Instead, we return laden with all sorts of provisions that have little or nothing to do with what we actually need. Whichever way we look, if we are honest, we can see how difficult it is for us to fulfill our original aim, and how easily we can be deflected, led off down some by-road, or even into a dead end, so that we have to turn right around and start all over again.

So often we go hither and thither, studying first this method and then that method, doing this exercise and that exercise, this practice and that practice. This can make us feel good for awhile, but all we are doing is placating our self-righteousness. But really, this has nothing to do with the work with which we could become involved. From the beginning of time, mankind has been given free choice. We can get what we want in life if we put our minds to it. In the end, if we have not put ourselves into the stream of service, which will bring us in touch with the real world, we will become ultimately disillusioned and may have to repeat the search all over again. It is only when we place ourselves in the stream of service by setting our intention *outside of time* that we can begin on what is called the way.

Let us examine what it could mean to make an intention outside of time. If we look at our own lives we will see that nearly all the intentions we have made have come about through comparison. It always involves a relationship with something that has already happened in our own lives, or in the lives of others. We decide to do something because of the pain we went through last time when we did something else. We make a decision to travel abroad because it is cold and foggy where we are. Everything is done in comparison to something else, as this world exists only because of the nature of duality. Yet our spiritual search is towards union, beyond comparison, beyond the mind, beyond discursive reasoning, beyond even consciousness itself.

It can be seen that, in order to come into the realization of unity, it is necessary to set our intention in a way that is not based on the conditioned mind or on the world of comparison and opposites. We can reach a place that lies exactly at the mid-point between this world and the world-to-come, between this world of illusion and the real world which is totally beyond description based on the mind. It is as though our intention is the bridge between the two worlds. The answer is in the question; and the intention is the eternal question asked of all mankind, the question which contains within itself the truth.

The moment we set our intention correctly, provided our motive is pure, we are immediately in the stream of service. We then can be led to where the Divine Will wishes us to go, where we can put our talents to the best possible use, where we can serve our fellow man in the knowledge and love of God.

Yet how hard it is! We are so cluttered with conditioning and preconceived notions as to what this spiritual path is all about that it is almost impossible for us to set the intention that will lead us and others towards the goal. That is why it is necessary to work on ourselves so that we can be more of service, more of help in the unfolding of the planet. With each conscious effort of work on ourselves, little by little the conditioning is melted away until finally we are clear enough to be totally committed to something that can neither be seen, nor felt, nor tasted, nor touched. The methods and the practices will help us toward this end perhaps, but no one but ourselves can make that commitment for us. If anyone says that he can, beware. It is too easy to give our wills into the hands of another, and thus lose the only opportunity we have of giving ourselves and surrendering ourselves completely into the knowledge of our essential unity with God. We have to take the plunge ourselves. No one can do it for us. Someone else can bring us right to the edge, but only we can drink from the fountain; only we can make that final act of commitment. To make that commitment requires courage, and integrity, and a pure motive, and, most of all, the passionate yearning to know God. Nothing less will suffice.

ASKING THE QUESTION *"It takes courage to ask a question and truly pay heed to the answer."*

It is said that in the question lies the answer. Therefore we would be foolish indeed if we did not ask a question. But it is not as simple as it sounds. First of all, we have to want to ask the question, then learn about the responsibility of taking action based on the answer and all that that implies. It is through asking a question from the heart that change may come about in the world, first in our so-called personal life, then with the family or group with which we work, and then finally, with the environment. A question implies that we both want to know the answer, and that we do not as yet know the answer. Here is another riddle. If we did not know the answer somewhere deep down inside, we would not ask the question in the first place.

Think of a scientist working in a laboratory, conducting a very complicated experiment. Perhaps he has been working on the experiment for many years. He has even brought in other scientists to help him complete the experiment and solve the riddle. To the outside world, he might appear as a crazy scientist wasting the tax-payer's money, but to the scientist himself, who first asked the question, it is quite another matter. He is setting out to prove something that he has already intuited to exist in one world or another. He has asked the question "Is this true, and if so, how can I help to manifest this knowledge in the relative world and in a practical way?"

In a sense, we first have to be taught just *how* to ask a question. That is seldom done. We too easily assume that we are going to be told something without doing anything about it. We need to prepare ourselves to receive what is necessary by truly opening our hearts to the question itself. We are liable to ask a question, and before we allow enough time to pass so that the answer may be given, we are already jumping ahead with another question, or perhaps even turning the question into a discussion. No profit can come from this. That is why it is so useful actually to be taught about the purpose of asking a question. Indeed, just *how* to ask it.

The first thing to understand is that whenever we communicate with each other correctly, there is an exchange of energy. What is communicated is energy itself manifested in the form of words. If we do not communicate with each other, there is just a chaotic movement of static, and no understanding can come from this. It is a matter of learning how to give and how to receive. How often do we actually do this correctly? If we are really honest with ourselves, we will find that even if we do ask questions, many times we are closed to the real answer that we are asked to comprehend. We take only the answer that we want, but seldom the answer that we need! Thus, there is no real exchange of energy, and certainly no transformation of energies.

It takes courage to ask a question and truly pay heed to the answer. Change lies within the answer, and there is always a part of us that does not wish to subscribe to change. That part of us is always content just to go on doing the same things over and over again. By repeating an old habit pattern, we can eventually stop change from coming about. A typical example of this can be seen in a room where someone is paying attention and asking a question which needs to be answered. The result would affect everyone there. If there is the slightest threat to the ego lying within the answer that may be given, immediately the level of noise in the room increases. Everyone starts speaking to everyone else at once, and all possibility of change coming about from the possibility of the answer is lost.

We need courage in order to be awake, both in asking and receiving. We need attention, that we may listen and, through the inner yearning of the heart, be awakened by will. After all, it is separation that brings about the very pain that we need to remind us continuously to turn back to the one Source of all life. From the highest level to the most practical level, all real questions come about from the pain of separation, the separation from the Answer.

If we really want to know who we are, remembering the words of the Prophet (may the peace and blessings of God be upon him), "He who knows himself, knows his Lord," there has to be a transformation of the lower energies. Our lower energies, or animal soul, cannot hear, and cannot ask questions. The animal soul has instinct, but no direct intuition. Therefore, we have to die to our lower natures by transforming them.

Suppose I heard that somewhere there was a very important book which would provide certain answers to a problem I had been working on for a long time. Then I found the right person to ask, who apparently knew the location of this book. At the same time, I was very tired and it was getting dark. The book was available in someone's house over the nearby hill. However, the person who owned the book was going away the following morning. The only way to get to the house was by walking through the forest that night. Now the lower nature would not, and could not, see the point of getting up and trudging several miles through the cold and dark to find a book. It would be necessary to have sufficient will at this point to get the body dressed, find a flashlight, and finally to set off on the long walk.

Assuming the higher nature won out over the lower nature, I would reach my destination, look through the book, and extract the answers I needed to complete the work in which I was involved. The lower nature, despite putting up all sorts of resistance to the idea, had actually helped in the process of getting the necessary answers. There would have been a subtle transformation of the energies involved. A higher energy (in this case, in the form of will) would have raised a lower energy, allowing room for still lower energies to be transformed when the time was right.

Thus, little by little, those aspects of ourselves which do not want to know the answer and are not yet even certain about the question, are transformed in a distillation process. Then, when it is possible for us to say, "Yes, I know who I am," the pain of separation will be over. For indeed, "He who knows himself, knows his Lord." At that moment we will at last be travellers on the way, lovers of God, and mystics in the true sense of the word. All of this comes about through holding the question always in our hearts. Let us never be so complacent that we presume that we know an answer without asking a question! Did not Jesus say, "Seek and ye shall find, knock and it shall be opened unto you"?

Words are a veil, and even consciousness itself is a veil. I wonder how often we come to question the nature of awareness. Who or what is God? How can we be aware of oneness, if there is only one God? Is it given to us on a plate? Can we just go about our daily lives and be aware of God? Or do we have to awaken to Him?

Every day of our lives, those of us who are seekers on the path wake up again to know that there is only one Being—not two Gods, or three Gods, or your God, or my God, but one absolute Being, one pure Light. But what is awareness? We place more stress on awareness than on anything else, because in order to come to Him, or to die to Him, to "die before death," we have to be awake to Him. In order to awaken, we have first to discover that we are asleep. Most of us go through all our lives and never know that we are asleep. We only think we are awake.

We imagine we can think a thought. If we really question ourselves on this idea, we will find that we can't think a single thought. Thought thinks us! But could we not come to be able to think a thought? Is this not what God, as the only creative Being, wishes for man to do? Can we become creative?

Man is a sleepwalker until he is awake, and sometimes he is more awake when he is asleep at night than when he is awake in the day! We find ourselves in great pain through the lifelong search for God, perhaps thinking that we can achieve something for Him.

Do we realize that most people go through the whole of their lives without ever asking a question? They have only thought that they have asked a question. Can we ever, unconditionally, ask that one great "Who am I?" Could we ask this so unconditionally that whatever it meant to us, even if it meant death, it would be the one important thing in this world that we could ask? Not "Who do I want to be?" or "Who do I want you to be?" but "Who am I?" If we do question, can we accept what we are, without any reservation whatsoever? Can we die before we die, die to everything we think we are? Awareness of God means to be awake to every moment of our lives, because the moment that we are awake it is the eternal Now. We, in these forms, are merely the continuum in eternity of one basic principle.

If we are awake, we cannot judge. When we judge another, we might say, "I like him or her, or this situation or that situation, but I don't like that part of it." We never accept oneness, so we can never be awake if we judge. Every teacher in the world from the beginning of time has said this. So the first stage in waking up to God is to understand what is meant by, "Judge not that ye be not judged." We have to learn to accept life exactly as it is, ourselves exactly as we are. We have to learn first of all to accept before we can do anything. How can we do this?

If we think about it, we realize how incredibly conditioned we are in life. We become conditioned from the moment we are born, when we are given a name. We are conditioned by parents, ancestors, education, conditioned by the very form that we are given. I am not saying these are wrong. I am just saying that we are conditioned. And all our words, which are just veils, are words explaining states of conditioning, states of our own conditioning. Words are veils. How can we lose this conditioning? Can we begin to lose the conditioning when we are eighty years old or do we have to start when we are a child? All these are questions we ask. The answer is in this moment. This moment is the only important moment we can ever know. Each moment is equally important, and each is the only moment because it will never come again.

Every moment we have to learn to be awake to God. God is one. It is necessary that we be awake to everything, not only what we want to be awake to.

There are different sorts of questions that we can ask at any one moment. It is up to us to be sufficiently attuned to ask the question correctly. The first sort, which I call a "personal question," is merely based on the past. There is nothing wrong with this. It is where we often start. A personal question has to do with the illusion of oneself as being separate from God. Most of the questions that we ask come from this illusion of separateness. I cannot say it is not valuable, but I can say that it does not produce what can be produced through the correct understanding of a question. For example, let us take the world of healing. When people come with a particular symptom, the healer will always try to put the question back to them in order that they might look at what it is and why the particular illness is manifesting itself. If the patient is prepared to listen, then both patient and healer can share something together. Often the patient will not, because it is always the personal question. It is always, "Me, Me," "It is my personal pain that my question is about." This can be useful, as long as we are strictly honest and someone is prepared to explain to us that by itself the personal question is useless. A personal question is based on the past, which has already gone.

The second sort of question is on a higher level and is based on our heart or soul's need. This is something quite different, because it is something which requires a greater degree of courage to ask. It might be, "What is the nature of will?" or "What is trust?" Even, "What is the purpose of life on Earth?" It is deeply personal, on the soul level, but is not personalized by our ego or our illusion of being separate from the unity of God. These questions are very important to ask, even if there is nobody in the physical form to give us an answer. We can ask these questions and receive an answer, as long as we go on asking the question and are prepared to wait for and accept the answer.

The third type of question directly involves the group or our family. Mr. Gurdjieff once said that it is practically impossible to do the work without a group, except on very rare occasions. Yet we must never rely on a group, because a group is individuals who have agreed to be together, not an excuse for not facing oneself. A group of individuals who choose to be together produce, in a sense, a vortex or empty center. It is not a matter of taking something, but a matter of what we give to it. How much we receive from a group is dependent upon how much we put into it. How much we give of our hearts in a question determines how much we receive. This is a very direct involvement. An example of this would be a question involving movement from one place to another, which directly concerns our family or group. You may think I am splitting hairs, but this is important. Not only do we need a tremendous sense of attunement and responsibility, of courage and inner authority, but we also need an enormous degree of compassion. We have to have compassion, because any question is going to produce some sort of answer, if asked correctly.

If we ask a question in service, it may not be for us alone to receive the answer, but somebody will receive it. If we are selfish about the answer, then we may get into terrible trouble. We so much want to see the answer manifested right in front of us, here and now. For example, I want pupils to understand everything I have been given. I want to give it all away, because there is no point in hanging onto it. I get so frustrated when people are not listening. Then I go to another town and discover that somebody whom I have never met has received the answer. We can understand that when a certain level is reached, that we all *can* reach, we are not involved with time/space relationships as we know them. The answer *has* been given, so asking a question is also an act of service which is very important.

The highest, the unspoken question I usually place in the upper reaches of consciousness, where it is heard and then takes time to filter down. We can hear it without any words. Something happens inside us. There is release, if you like. Sometimes we cry. Eventually the result will filter down and permeate our lives, and from that we may take action.

This level of question comes about from the knowledge that in the question lies the answer. The question in this case is manifested through a certain attention and continuous yearning from the heart. To have this attention we must be completely awake and attuned to the higher worlds beyond the mind and even beyond consciousness itself. It is the attention of the mystic whose heart has finally opened to the divine mysteries. When the attention and the yearning fuse together, they produce a question somewhere in the world, in someone else. That is why it is said, "If you pronounce His Name correctly, immediately someone is turning towards God."

In normal life it is difficult to know just where a question comes from. We are always so identified with what "we" are (or rather think we are) that we forget, not yet having the necessary attention, that the question is always here if we can only be open to it. Finally, we realize that we are merely instruments through which the question can be asked and through which the question can be answered.

If there were no true mystics in the world, no one would ask a real question! That is why Mevlana Jelaluddin Rumi, the thirteenth century mystic, talks about the path of the mystic being so vital. It is not more important than any other path. Everything is needed for the answer to the question to be manifested upon Earth. But it is vital, for it contains the *elan vital*, the elixir of life, the philosopher's stone that helps transform the base metals into gold.

THE NEED FOR REAL CHANGE *"When we commit ourselves to the Work, which is sometimes called the Spirit of God, we commit ourselves, once and for all, to change."*

There is change, and there is the apparency of change. If we make our commitment to the Work, which is sometimes called "the Spirit of God," we commit ourselves, once and for all, to change. We commit ourselves, first of all, to allow ourselves to be changed, and then to being an agent for real change to take place in the world around us—in our family, our friends, in society, and in the world as a whole. It is no good pretending to have committed ourselves to the Work if we are not prepared to accept change and all that it brings with it. It is not useful to put one foot on the path and leave another on the old road. It is not useful, and it can also be dangerous. Real change may then come about before we are prepared for all that this entails.

When we commit ourselves to the Work, we commit ourselves, once and for all, to change. There is no way out. There is no back door through which we can escape. We have made our commitment *outside of time,* and thus have set out on what is called "the path of service." We have truly become channels for necessary change—but change when the time is right, when everything is properly prepared.

This principle is illustrated in nature. Without the cycles of change, the planet itself could not live and give us life. It is because of change, and therefore through comparison, that life exists at all. Each season gives way to another season. It does not fight the necessity of change, but just gives way, bows to the next stage, welcomes it home. Spring gives way to summer, summer to autumn, autumn to winter. And as the cycle goes on and on, year after year, generation after generation, the seasons offer us again and again the possibility of learning what is necessary.

Let us look at it this way. One year we plant potatoes and the next year, during the same season, we plant corn on the same land. Each crop brings about a different set of circumstances, yet each one follows the natural flow of the seasons. If potatoes were planted in the same field during the same season each year, slowly the soil would be depleted, the potato crop would fail, and there would be wastage. Crop rotation provides new food for the soil and new types of harvest for those who sow. Thus within the laws governing the cycles of life we see the apparency of change. One year we plant this crop, and another year we plant that. The situation seems to be different, yet it is only following the laws that govern the seasons of the year. The laws governing the seasons remain the same. The differences that we see are merely different manifestations of the same principle.

With knowledge of these laws, we can really be of service and help to give back what we have been given. The land will be able to produce more to support human beings who, potentially, have within themselves the means of bringing about the true change that is necessary, thus fulfilling their responsibility in being born man and woman.

When Mr. Gurdjieff said, "Life is real only then, when I AM," he left it to his readers to interpret this statement on the level that each person was working from—that level being dependent on the amount of work the individual had done on himself. Now perhaps we can look at the meaning behind these words so that the understanding of *how* change comes about can be more real for us.

"The One divides in order to unite." This concept is familiar from many traditions. What we wish to look at here is just how the One does divide. The cause of creation is love. God is love. There is a saying in the *hadith* of the Prophet Mohammed (may the peace and blessings of God be upon him), "I was a hidden treasure and I longed to be known; so I created the world that I might be known." God divides Himself that He may be known.

How does this come about? It is essentially very simple. The moment we say "I" there is immediate and spontaneous separation. Now if we follow the *via negativa,* the way that is based upon negation of the illusion and of that which creates the illusion (i.e., the false "I" that feels it is separate from the unity of all life), then we understand this process as creating a sense of separation of the individual from his or her Creator. Paradoxically, in the path of negation we affirm separation by the assumption that there is anything to negate. In reality, separation is always an illusion, for there is only one Being.

He said, "I was a hidden treasure, and I longed to be *known."* How would it be possible for anything to be known, and for that knowledge to be confirmed, if there were not the illusion of separateness? If there were no mirror, how could we see ourselves? If there were not the exterior world, the outward form, would there be any chance of knowing the hidden that lies within what we apparently see? In this world it is necessary that there be a vehicle through which and within which there may be knowledge, so that an apparent world of duality can be brought into the realization of unity.

The apparency of separation, of duality, is necessary for the creative process to unfold. Although the way of negation, aimed at bringing us to a desireless state, is a very real way, it is only one half of the picture. The way of the Work in the West is the way of affirmation, but this is made possible only through the way of negation that has gone before. First comes the way of negation, and then comes the way of affirmation. First comes the realization of who and what we are through the discovery that all that we thought we were is illusion (thought being a process that is already past, already gone); and then comes the affirmation of what we really are and thus the beginning of the next stage of the Work.

In the Work, we come to know that it is through affirmation, made possible only by negation, that real change can come about. The moment that real change does occur we are subject to a totally new set of laws. We have free choice. We can revert to the old set of laws which brought us to the point of negation, or we can make ourselves ready to understand another set of laws that are available to us through committing ourselves to saying "I am." "Life is real only then, when I AM." Life is made real only when we come to affirm the presence of God by saying "I AM" We are not stating that there is separation, but affirming the whole creative process by stating the very word that brings that process into manifestation! "I AM"—because I know that I am one with God. "I AM"—because I know that He needs me to affirm Him by saying "I." Through that affirmation He divides Himself in order to unite. A mirror is made; a comparison takes place; a need is created; a desire is born in man. And so we see the ongoing process of evolution.

If we enter the path, and are accepted as a worker in this process that we call life, then it is necessary that we know about the different laws to which we can give affirmation from our own hearts. If we are merely living in the world, being processed by the world, seeking out an existence in the world, then we can quite easily define the laws that control and govern our lives. We might, for example, look at the different laws of the country in which we live, or the laws of the society, or the rules within the family. We can realize that we are subjected to the gravitational pull of the moon, and see how our birth, and (potentially) all that comes after birth, has some dependence on the movements of the planets. Every way we look we will be able to find these laws. It is even possible to study them and, through the knowledge of them, to live a relatively balanced life. Through following the laws of the family, the society in which we live and work, and the country we have chosen to make our home, we can find the most harmonious way of living in that society.

But supposing we enter the path of service? Supposing we come upon the Work, the manifestation of the Spirit of God, which is involved with bringing about real change? What then? When we enter this path we actually put ourselves in touch with an entirely different set of laws. We would be foolish if we did not study them and work with them for our own harmony and the harmony of those around us.

Once we truly want to understand what the Work is about, we can no longer revert to the old way of life. There is no point in following the laws of the country we have just left and trying to impose them on the country to which we have come! There are different circumstances here, and different considerations based upon different needs. We make our journey to this new world that we have chosen and then, in humility, we ask of those who already live in that place what rules they have found to help fulfill the natural order of life. Only if we ask can we possibly learn what is required of us and thus find out how we can be of service.

The average man is subject to the laws that govern life as we seem to experience it in this world. These laws arise out of "want" and "desire"—wanting something for myself, for example—the desire to do this or that which is directly related to the word "me." Yet, it is not the "I" which knows the purpose of that affirmation. It is the "I" that feels itself separate from everything else, and which continues a process of the apparency of change. It is not the "I" that knows, through affirmation, that it is participating in the evolutionary process itself.

For those who enter upon the path of service, there are two sets of laws. There are the laws based upon want and desire, but now we are subject also to laws based upon *need*. This is what we are asked to consider—the meaning of the word "need" and all that it implies.

Through negation we discover what we, as individuals, do not need. We find out that the things we thought we needed were not truly necessary. We might have *wanted* them, and we might still want them, but we do not *need* them any more.

So through the *via negativa* we discover that want and need are two entirely different concepts. Want and desire arise each moment of our lives in the relative world. Real need is God's need. It is the need for us to turn to Him alone, and thus to be able to know what needs to be done in order to fulfill an aspect of the divine order. Need is based upon time—not the time we create from our own desires, but the time resulting from the natural flow of life itself. The need is established before time as we experience it. Night and day, sun and moon, the turn of the seasons are the first stages of the unfolding of a principle that existed before time. After these stages appears a series of laws that govern the real world—first, the law of three forces, and then, the sevenfold work of the octave of life. The planet tilts on its axis while orbiting the sun, creating the seasons. Awakened man, conscious man, becomes the agent to bring the next two great laws into manifestation.

God is love and love becomes relative only when we desire, when we want, and when we apply the word "I" to life. The false "I" is made of the substance created out of desire. Yet if there were no desire, the love of God could not unfold itself into the relative world. This is perhaps one of the greatest paradoxes for the aspirant on the path. We are asked to give up our desire and to come to understand the real world. Yet God needs for us to say "I" if there is to be any change, any on-going process in our world. God needs man to say "I," having affirmed his unity with God in saying "I AM," so that life has, at last, become real for him.

Desire is relative, love is absolute. The former without the latter is impossible. Without our desire, our yearning, love cannot continue to break out of unity and bring about the miracle of diversity. God *needs* for us to want to know Him and thus to be awake to the laws that govern real change within the cycles set before time.

To be one of those who follow "the way" is a very great honor and privilege, but it is hard sometimes to understand what this could mean. There are no rewards that are given. There is no great joy in the early stages. Often when we look around at the different schools and paths, we find it easy to doubt, when so many appear to be singing and dancing and all seems to be so fine. Let me try to explain what the way is all about.

It is not a path of self-development; it is a path of sacrifice. It is not a path that is strewn with flowers or glamor; it is honest-to-God hard work. It is ruthlessly demanding and if we are chosen to be on this path, it is a rare case when the Good Lord lets him go! "I want only you," He says, and that is indeed the case. It is not a path of form. It is not even a path of the formless, for that, too, is a concept. The way requires courage and perseverance in the face of what seem to be almost insurmountable difficulties. The way requires that we consider nothing as more important than what we are asked to do. The way is fulfilling the purpose of life on Earth.

Our obligation is to find out the way, to seek it out in everything that we see, feel, think, or do. Let us now look below the surface of things and never accept things at their face value. May we be intelligent, that is, to awaken intelligence through will, the Spirit. We no more see a chair, for instance, as just a chair, nor even as a pattern of shapes and molecular structure, but rather as a manifestation of the Divine. That is the way.

The way is not easy. It has existed from the beginning of time and was neither born, nor created. It permeates all things, gives life to all things, and yet is independent of all things. To seek out the way we must learn to love very, very much. The first thing we are asked to do is to learn to love the plant and mineral kingdoms and, of course, all of God's creation. Only when we have come to love these aspects of the kingdom of God can we be said to be able to participate in conscious love itself. We might be able to love our neighbors as ourselves. If we sing with the plants, we may awaken to God's beauty in the plants. Remember, "The sole purpose of love is beauty." Do we not yet see that the plants are loving us all the time? But we do not often see this. We take things too much for granted. Nothing, I repeat, nothing must be taken for granted if we are to keep on the way, the straight way that leads to freedom.

To love each other in the Name of God! Now, here is the greatest challenge of all, for who is loving whom? Are we really separate from each other, or are we just exemplars of the unity of God? The mind can conjure up all sorts of splendid ideas, but it is only the heart that can truly understand. We are asked to polish the mirror of the heart. We do this by knocking at the door of the heart, remembering that the door is opened from the inside. We ourselves cannot open it. So who opens it? Only when we can say, "It is Thou," in answer to His question, "Who is knocking at My door?" that the door can be opened.

If we go beyond the mind (which, in one sense, is necessary for the world of comparison to exist), then what happens to "us"? I mean, what happens to what we thought we were in the first place? Where will all the sacred cows go, and the caterpillars that we wanted to turn into butterflies? What would happen if we simply ceased to exist as a concept? What is there beyond the concept of who and what we are? No one can tell us that!

If no one can tell us the truth but Truth itself, then how do we proceed? We can seek all the time, keeping the question in the heart and mind all the time, and not give up. If there is no one who can tell us the truth, then from where does the answer come?

If we do everything for love, in love, and by love, all that stands in the way of the truth of love goes, little by little. Even "Reason is powerless in the expression of love!"

Meditation in love melts the stuff of mind, so, little by little, we are left with nothing to hang onto. It is at that stage that we really turn, once and for all, to our Lord. There is nothing else to do! When we have realized that the only road to service is sacrifice itself, we can go on. To be wounded in love is to see the battle won.

This path is not for the squeamish or half-hearted. It is not for the arrogant or the selfish. It is not for those who want half the truth. It is for those who are chosen by God to come to know Him, and to know of His ways. And only in complete humility can we approach the door of the heart. We approach the door of the heart when there is nothing else to do. When we knock properly, it shall be opened unto us. That is the promise that we were given, and are given, from the beginning of time. Finally, we may know there is only Him. We are veiled by endless masquerades, until the right time comes for the veils to be lifted, and we can see Him face to face, and truly say, "Oh Thou!"

We have free choice. We can remain in a tight knot of illusion, governed by the old laws based upon want and desire, or we can begin to learn from those who have already seen into the real world. We can know the laws that are necessary for a new order to come on Earth. The East has traditionally followed the way of negation. Now the West, through all that has gone before, is asked to follow the path of affirmation *in the knowledge of the unity of God,* knowing that in saying "I AM" life becomes real for the first time. Thus we begin to fulfill our destiny in being born man and woman. When humanity is established, we know that all people, from whatever race or creed, will come to the wonderful realization that we are all one within this Divine Principle.

CONSCIOUS LOVE

C ONSCIOUS LOVE *"Our responsibility in being human is to come to understand that we are placed into this universe, on this planet, in order to know how to love."*

Our attitude to love must be conscious. For it to be conscious, we must study the nature of love. We may discover that love is the cause of all creation. In our relationships with each other we are linked through our love for each other to the greatest force in the universe. Love itself is absolute. It cannot be defined or measured, seen, felt, or heard. The force of love, the cause of all creation, is the flowing out from the Absolute to our relative existence. This flow, and the quality and quantity of the flow, is dependent upon the vehicle through which that force of love flows. Our responsibility in being human is to come to understand that we are placed into this universe, on this planet, in order to know how to love. It is only through the perfected man that the perfect law of God can be brought to Earth. It is only through perfected man that heaven can come on Earth, this planet that so desperately needs to be loved, just as it gives its life continuously to us, to our life here.

People do not realize the need for conscious love because they do not, as yet, want to love consciously. They want to be taken by the experience brought about in the state of love. They wish to be swept along in the force of love, not wishing to be real human beings, who are responsible for what passes through them.

Let us explore this word love. We can say, "God is love"— but is that enough? "God needs man"—how else is the divine law going to be made manifest on Earth? People have said, "Just leave it to God, or love"—but is that enough? We might say, "God is pure energy." But energy is neutral, and can come and go in any way we let it. The energy release when two or more are gathered together in the name of God is vast, but it can be used in any way. We can waste it, and it is said that this is the only sin, on any level we want to take it. We can turn it to so-called good, or so-called bad. Both are relative concepts, because in the absolute state there is not good or bad.

However, we can, in knowledge, apply love or energy. That is the responsibility of being born man and woman. "Man is a cosmic transformer of subtle energies." That is what we are, but most people want to believe only what they *feel* they are. What we think we are is certainly not what we are, because we are not our thoughts. And what we think somebody else is is not what they are; that's merely a projection. The only thing that divides us is thought or combinations of thought. Nothing else divides us. I might judge you, or you judge me, and we get into division. As my beloved teacher once said to me, "When you judge another, you humiliate the other and veil yourself."

In the Sufi tradition, there are four turns toward love. The first turn is hearing the possibility of a new life. We hear something of what life could be. If we're sensitive enough, and awake at that moment, we may go looking for it. God gives us free choice. And, at that point, we are offered two possibilities. We can attempt to take the old laws from our previous ignorance into our future, or discard those laws and move into something new. And if we are lucky enough at that time to have somebody to help us, as I have been lucky to have people help me, we will learn that we cannot take all the laws of the old age into the new age. Without help, we could split ourselves up the middle. In the first turn, we hear about the possibility of a new world, in ourselves, in our family, in the planet as a whole. We then have free choice, and may go on to the second turn. We can only come to it by giving up everything that we were before meeting up with that moment. At the moment we give up, we come into the second turn. That is our first taste of being, being within Being. To come into this turn, we have to give up the first experience. And that is the step towards the third turn. To get to this next one, they say we have to give up all knowledge, all concepts, and absolutely everything, in the trust of God. We know that, in essence, in each one of us and everywhere, there is the possibility of perfection and perfect order. The third turn is called conviction. It is possible we can become totally convinced, not only in the outward and visible signs, but in our own living experience, within ourself. These three turns are the three steps leading to the fourth, the last turn, in which there is no more separation between God and man. I and my Father are one. There is just He.

These are the steps that we may come to if we begin to become awake, whether we know it in this life, or in one moment (for there is only this moment), or whether we see it one day, or whether we see it in our children. Every moment we are conscious, every moment we pray consciously, every moment we breathe consciously, with everything we do consciously, we are dying to what we thought we were. And every moment we die to what we thought we were, certain energy is released which goes toward the future of mankind. If we keep awake, we can do anything in five minutes, or two minutes, or one minute, or no time at all, because we have decided to do it in this time, the only amount of time we have to get it done. This is a key. You, I, your children, and my children, have the power of decision. The tragedy of it is, we don't know it until we know we're asleep, and want to wake up.

What is choice? How can we make choices in life if we are conditioned in the slightest? Every single choice we make is based on our own conditioning. Everything is based upon the degree of conditioning, of what we think this is, or what we think that is. Only when we are free of conditioning can we make a choice consciously; only then. I know it sounds horrific, but it is true. I could help you to recondition your conditioning, and you might be very happy with it. I'm afraid to say this is often done. But suppose you are on your death bed, completely and utterly on your death bed, all the games the mind can play and all the courses that teachers will sell you are just total illusion, total sadness and frustration. Then, of course, it is a question of courage. Can you face it and see what it means to be alive?

If we are really honest with ourselves, we will find that it is rare that we totally inhabit our bodies, these vehicles which

God has given us to manifest His Will on Earth. We are offered this challenge to see if we can be truly awake to the present moment and thus able to manifest whatever needs to be done in any one moment. The lower nature of ourselves does not want to listen, and, in fact, until a very great transformation of energy takes place, is incapable of listening. Thus, work on the transformation of the lower energies is an essential part of our life if we truly wish to be of service.

People often ask me, "Well, how can I be awake?" My reply is often, "Are you here?" At the moment they asked the question, obviously they were not totally here, inhabiting their bodies. Otherwise, there would have been no question, since the real question is dependent upon being right here in the present moment. What my teachers have stressed is that it is all to do with the matter of respect. In the highest level, we could say that it is the respect of God that makes us want to work. If we did not trust that there is one absolute Being, or if we did not wish to know the truth, then there would be no reason why we should attempt to work on ourselves.

It is true that respect needs to be given whole-heartedly to a teacher, but, as I said before, it is a question of being awake to the need, and realizing that the teacher is merely another function of God. His or her presence in the material world is only because of need. If there were no need for knowledge, then there would be no teachers. It is because of our inner yearning and need that a teacher can appear amongst us, fulfilling that particular function within the overall plan of God.

Man, we say in this tradition, is made of fire, earth, air, water, and ether. In the cosmos, there are the four kingdoms: the mineral kingdom, the vegetable kingdom, the animal kingdom, and man. Everything is within man. There is nothing outside of man. All truth is within and understood, as we learn to breathe with God. I know that the breath is the most important of all ways, of all things, to do in order to become awake. After all, we came in on the breath and we will die on the breath. But when are we awake to breathe?

Can we, in love, breathe together? It is almost totally

forgotten in the churches and in our training. But can we breathe together? Each of us is interpenetrated with all the thoughts and judgments of each other, and the love, the light, and all the things apparently good and apparently bad. Like the waves of the sea these move through us on the breath. So can we learn to breathe with God?

If we can learn to breathe with God, we can learn to communicate with Him in all His aspects. We can communicate even with the mineral world, because it has consciousness, and with the vegetable world, the animal world. We can know the needs of Him who is in all things.

To be awake we have to want to love God more than anything else. It is an unconditional surrender. "Reason is powerless in the expression of love. Love alone is capable of revealing the truth of love and of being a lover. The way of our prophets is a way of truth. If you want to live, die in love. Die in love if you want to remain alive." This was said by one of the great mystics of all time, Mevlana Jelaluddin Rumi. God is Love. How can we die consciously while we are still alive, die to every moment, carry nothing with us, want nothing, yearn for nothing in acceptance of union with God? I know we can do it only if we look through the veils, not with dogma but through dogma, not at form but within the essence of the form. I feel it is a question of surrender, not of achievement. We cannot achieve the truth. Knowledge cannot be acquired; it can only be given.

In order to be awake to God, we have to understand that He, in His perfection, always has been and always is perfect. Therefore, since everything is within, there is nothing to achieve!

We talk about light, the light of God. We've been chasing after the light and chasing after God. But do we realize that light does not travel at 186,000 miles per second, as scientists say it does? That's only a relative explanation. Light, like God, unfolds from itself. He, that one Being, unfolds from His Essence in every single moment. All we have to do to know Him is to surrender to Him. Surrender everything that we think we are, everything that we want to be, everything we ever thought we were, and then God, or Light, or Love unfolds from within.

We all long to be respected. He wishes in His prayer for us that we awaken to the essence within each of His creatures. Without respect, we cannot be awake to the needs of the moment manifesting in His creatures. It is easy to see how little we respect the Mother Earth, how we continue to rape the planet in our greed and ignorance. It is sometimes harder to realize how little we respect each other. As we study more and more, we begin to be given certain knowledge which allows us to understand our purpose, to respect on deeper and deeper levels. If we study the meaning of esoteric prayer, we will discover before long that the degree to which we can help is dependent upon our degree of knowledge. Therefore, the question of knowledge is really the first step along the path.

Once again, in order to be awake, it is necessary to realize that we are asleep most of the time. If I say this to some people, they become very resentful. It is our degree of resentment, envy, and pride that separates us from the truth. We can work on these matters, to make sacrifices so that our lower self may be subjected to will and led into the present moment. Without will, there is no possibility of this.

Let us consider the analogy of training a wild horse. First, we have to find the horse, and catch it, before we can put a halter around its neck. The horse does not like any of these actions initially, because it does not know its purpose. We have to train the horse to walk with a "regular pace." If it is to be a show horse or racehorse, we have to have the necessary knowledge to teach the horse in a special way what is required of it. We have to put a saddle on the back of the horse, which it dislikes even more. Although up to this point we can have several assistants in the training process, at the moment we mount onto the saddle, we are alone. There then is a period that is entirely dependent upon our strength and will. If these are sufficient, we will be able to break the horse in and ride it. Finally, it may take us to our destination.

When we have controlled our lower natures, we then have something to offer the Master—the Judge—the Arbitrator.

To complete the analogy of a horse, when we have trained the horse sufficiently, we may take it into the show ring, beautifully poised and ready. We are then tested. "We will try them until we know." Finally, the judge of the ring makes his decision. Perhaps it has taken us many years to train the horse. At last we are able to lead it into the show ring—the present moment. As I keep stressing, our lower nature does not know that it is asleep. Hopefully, we can now see that it is from our lower nature that the degrees of resentment, envy, and pride manifest. To realize we are asleep may bring us to want very, very much to be awake. As we begin to awaken, we begin to see the necessity of respect in every aspect of life. Respect then opens us to knowledge, and knowledge leads us to love. Thus, through work on ourselves, we are answering God's prayer until, finally, we can be granted the workings of prayer itself.

FOUR PRECEPTS: REMEMBRANCE, MEDITATION, TRUST, AND SERVICE

"Learn to turn to each person as the most sacred person on Earth, to each moment as the most sacred moment that has ever been given to us."

We can be helped by certain basic precepts that come in all the major traditions. The Sufi endeavors to follow these precepts at all times. While he goes about his daily work, he is engaged in the remembrance of God, meditation, trust, and service. Since all of creation is in a single moment, all of these qualities are potentially available to us in the eternity of the now. It may be necessary to clarify these in greater depth. Then, we may begin to live our lives in accord with a greater sense of purpose.

We can be helped by having certain basic precepts that come in all the major traditions. The first thing is to remember God, all our lives, in every moment of our lives. To do that, we are asked to be awake to God; we must learn to breathe with God. We must learn to love Him with all the parts of our being, all parts, not just the bits that we want. So the first thing is remembering God, every moment.

It is this attitude of awareness, or "self-remembering," which moves us along the path of return. For in awakening to what is present, we recognize who we are, and what we may become. Perhaps we remember the source of our own life. The Sufis have certain exercises for remembrance (called *zikr*), some of which are involved with saying *Allah* with every breath or every step they make. Ordinary man uses only a portion of his potential because he is asleep, forgetful of his real nature. He consents to run his life mechanically, moved through the world by the force of events beyond his awareness or control. It is only when a man awakens to himself in the present moment that he can even begin to realize his relationship to God. It is no good thinking that he is awake, because the very act of thought divides him from his rightful place in the eternal now. He is asked always to remember to stay linked to his Source. Whatever thoughts do arise in that moment are seen as realizations emerging from eternity to provide the conditions necessary for action to be taken. Therefore, the exercise of remembering is actually useful in the living of life, particularly if the person is concerned with living a useful life.

The second quality of living could be called "meditation." This is commonly misunderstood. Meditation which ignores the remembrance stage is almost totally useless. It tends to take the person away from the present moment where the action is possible. It is insufficient simply to achieve a state of calm and detachment in the midst of life, for without the awareness of the self we are given the work will not be completed. There will be a lack of purpose in our lives. Awareness of God is necessary if we are to come to realize the responsibility we have in being man and woman.

Meditation is a form of self-imposed discipline which serves to keep the vehicle clear. Water takes on the color of the vessel which contains it. We purify our own vessel so that the "water" of love may flow through us into the world, to serve in the reciprocal maintenance of the planet. Meditation is not for "self-development," which is much misused as an expression. If we do not know what the "self" is, how can we develop it? If we try to develop ourselves, we may just put new coats on the vehicle instead of clearing it.

Meditation does not necessarily mean sitting on our backsides in the traditional way. Life itself is meditation. Somebody said to me the other day that there is no difference between the sacred and the secular. How can we say that God is in one thing and not in another? How can we say that we can only find God by closing our eyes? Life itself is meditation, and in order to understand that, we have to accept all life.

Meditation should be an act of love, accompanied by that joyous freedom which comes when we surrender to God to enable His Will to be done. It can be done while sitting peacefully alone or in the midst of our daily life, in every waking moment when we can surrender ourselves to Him, to His Will, to the need of the moment. With the attitude of meditation, our life can become a dance of joy, filled with the realization that our life is being given to the fulfillment of a greater plan. What more joy can there be than this?

Meditation is an art which needs to be learned step by step. As we practice remembrance and purification of action, we awaken a dormant quality of trust within ourselves. It is the attitude of trust that provides the third aspect of the spiritual guidelines. The ability to trust can be clouded or veiled by guilts and fears. Every sort of consideration about ourselves also takes us away from the present moment and keeps us from seeing the truth. But we can again come into truth, through a continual process of recognition that all actions could indeed be God's actions. For this to happen, we need to learn how to accept without judgment, for when we judge another human being we humiliate the person we judge, and at the same time we veil ourselves. Every time we judge, it is like throwing a ball against a wall. The ball bursts and instantaneously bounces back to cover us like an invisible sticky substance that blocks the heart. This is how we build up karma every day. "Judge not that ye be not judged."

The third precept is trust. When we come to trust God and

His appearance in every moment, we begin to recognize the guidance and presence which is always with us and is exemplified by the great saints and prophets and scriptures of all times. This message is presented in various names and forms according to what is needed at a given time and place. It is surely necessary that we open ourselves to the perception of this knowledge through practices of prayer and invocation and especially through study and inquiry. Words can act as the carrying force of truth, once we have learned how to ask for guidance and listen for the answer in our hearts. When we learn to trust the inner perception of the truth, we become able to act more in accordance and harmony with the universal laws.

In order to trust we have to respect, not only each other, but all the kingdoms of life, the planet itself, the whole universe. When we can learn to trust unconditionally in the one God and all His messengers, we are led to faith. This is not faith that is blind, but living faith. It is the faith of the gnostic, who knows that there is one God and knows that he knows. If he has this faith, he can come into a complete conviction in God and then eventually reach a state of "abandonment." In the state of abandonment the gnostic can no longer say, "I believe in God," because he has already died to himself and knows only God. "O Father, take away the 'I am' from me and Thee until there is only Thee."

Without this quality of trust, our understanding is limited to that which we hang on to and that which we want to believe in, which is always only a partial truth. If we set ourselves up to decide what is true and false, we are competing with God. We are going against the greatest force in the universe, which is love unfolding in each moment, and we may end up getting hurt. Trust is necessary if we are to take any steps out of our bondage. That trust must be absolute and unconditional. He wishes us to know Him as He is. Once we have set foot on the path, it is inevitable that we should come to meet Him, if we trust the process. Once we have tasted the water of life, nothing can remain except the yearning in the heart for union with the Beloved.

The fourth quality is to dedicate our lives to service of God and humanity. We dedicate ourselves as vessels remembering our purpose, purified and emptied, in the trust that the waters of life will pour through us to sustain life on the planet. We dedicate ourselves at the moment we turn towards God and say, "I will." From that moment on we are given exactly what we need.

This last stage is to be able to be of service to God in full consciousness. We no longer can say at that point, "Thy will be done." Instead we say, "Let Thy wish become my desire." We can only be there in full service when we are not there! This is the way in which we try to come to awareness of God. And this is why it doesn't matter which religion somebody comes from, what background. It doesn't matter who we are, because there is only one God. Learn to turn to each person as the most sacred person on Earth, to each moment as the most sacred moment that has ever been given to us. This moment may never happen again, because no two moments are ever alike. Are we perhaps awake a bit more, perhaps breathing together with God? If we are awake, then love can flow and, as we turn once more to God, a complete transformation can take place in human beings. We can come through love of God to be of real service to humanity, in unconditional surrender.

All four of these precepts interpenetrate and may coexist in the present moment. All four are necessary all the time for us to lead a useful spiritual life. Living the spiritual life is to live the natural and normal way in the world, not always to be trying to escape from life. Natural is the same as spiritual, and they both mean being one with the flow of life itself. Now, as you read this, this moment, the flow of life is happening. Divine energy is being poured into the world exactly according to the needs of this moment. All appearances are the language of the divine energy expressing its truth as a realization of itself so that all can share in it.

Every moment is different, because God never expresses Himself twice in the same moment. There is a continuous re-creation in each moment. "Time is the eternal attribute of God," as the Sufis say. He is temporal in this world and eternal in the eternal now. To live the spiritual life is to be able to allow the eternal to express itself through us into the present moment, without its being unduly colored by our own inner veils. These veils distort the appearance and block the flow of life essence wishing to manifest itself.

How should we conduct our lives in order to fulfill the obligation inherent in being human? We have been taught to pray and do various exercises which prepare us to be of service for the divine plan, but we still yearn for the day which will bring us into freedom. In our hearts, if we are truly seeking, we form a question, which becomes an inner prayer that motivates us and calls us forward. As a great dervish once told me, "The world is full of your prayers; now all we need is love." It is that love which will permit the answer to our prayers to become manifest.

What is the purpose of prayer at this time? To whom and to what should we be praying? Can we pray anymore to some unknown force or God who will provide us with all the answers? If we really recognize that there is one absolute Being, prayer would be seen in a different light. For when we are turning towards that one Source of all life, it is only a matter of opening ourselves in love so that the flow of that life is facilitated. The answer to our prayer may then appear anywhere, according to the will of God. Prayer then becomes a relaxation within the one Being which allows His will or life force to flow to where it is needed. This flow is primarily the flow of love.

We are looking at the possibility of a new understanding of the nature of prayer and devotion in our time without losing the simplicity and sincerity of the past thousands of years. We wish to come into knowledge of how prayer can be useful in the scheme of things.

To pray is to ask a question. There is really only one question and only one prayer, from which all else follows. We can contact that essential yearning of all creatures, which is the yearning of God. If we come to that yearning, and find the meaning of that yearning in our own life, we will find out the meaning of the one prayer, asking the one question. If we ask the one question sincerely, we will find the one answer, which is the prayer contained within the question.

God willing, there comes a time in the life of all of us when we are brought to our knees. At this point there is nothing more important than the truth. From the depths of the yearning in our hearts, in desperation, we will turn to ask for the way that will guide us to the only possible satisfaction in our lives, which is the realization of union with God.

One day, when "the time is fulfilled," we will see Christ in every babe. But this can only come about when we dedicate our lives to the bringing of God's Will on Earth as it is in Heaven, in order to truly fulfill our obligation in being man and woman.

"When two or three are gathered together in My Name, there am I, in the midst of them . . ."

The responsibility inherent in being man and woman is to be able to say the word "I," then to say "I AM," and finally to say "I WILL." Prayer and devotion, and the constant yearning of the heart, will bring us to partake of that responsibility. The four guidelines of remembrance, meditation, trust, and service will act as the framework for the expression of our goodwill. All we need is sufficient love and devotion actually to do it. Let us pray that we will all come to surrender our lives in service so that we may be filled with life.

The Prayer of Abandonment
Father, into Thy hands I abandon myself.
Do with me whatever You will and whatever You do
I will thank You and remain always grateful.
Let only Thy will be done in me as in all Your creatures.
Into Thy hands I commit my spirit; I give it to You
with all the love of my heart, for I love You, Lord,
and so long to give myself with a trust beyond all measure.

FREEDOM
"The true heritage of the soul is freedom."

The wisdom contained in all history can be revealed to us in the way that we need it. All creation, in reality, is in one moment, but then goes on unfolding itself until the end of time. If we could truly come to understand the real message brought to humanity by the great masters and prophets, then eventually all that has been contained in the past would be brought into the present moment. Like Solomon in his time, we would have control over our own destiny; and as in the self-sacrifice of Jesus, we would be in total service to God. Each of the great masters reveals a certain quality of the one great Source.

In Sufism we talk about *Fana* and *Baqa*. *Fana* is the passing away of illusion and *Baqa*, the remaining of the essential truth. Various practices can help dissolve the false nature of the limited "I" consciousness. Little by little, the hidden life within each of us can start to be revealed. Often there are great moments of rapture and wonder as we surrender to the stream of life force, but the knowledge of who and what we are often eludes us. What we are, in essence, is all things, all past time, and the infinite possibility of the future. But the New Jerusalem that we build within ourselves is made of the bricks of real knowledge, not of shifting sand. As we learn to love God more and more, we become more and more one with Him in the realization that really there was never any separation.

The true heritage of the soul is freedom. It is the birthright we were given from the beginning of time. The obligation we have in being man and woman, the link between Heaven and Earth, is to bring into this world the knowledge which is creating this world each moment. We must anchor this great force of love through knowledge so that what is needed is brought into this world for the generations to come—for the actual planet itself.

It is said that some people are destined to know God and some are destined to know God and His ways. We can know

Him in His oneness and in the miracle of His attributes, which are numberless.

First of all, I think we can understand that thought influences our lives. Once a thought has gone into the relative world, it can never die. We may think it is dead or has disappeared, but it cannot really die once the vibration has been set up. It is, as it were, collected by other human beings in the form of the written word or in the form of an opinion, which then spreads like a forest fire. The original thought may change as it spreads from person to person or group to group, but it has not died. There is another form of thought vibration which we experience as emotional sensation. It is easy to label an emotion fear, grief, or anger, but it is not so easy to understand the subtle nature of emotion, which is also a form of vibration and hence never dies. We can also understand that there are higher forms of emotion, such as yearning, which cannot really be understood at all. The yearning of the soul upwards in prayer, the yearning for freedom, also does not die. There are other types of higher vibration as well, from which we are continuously becoming.

If these vibrations do not die, where do they go? This is the great key to understanding how there is an alternative way of life within society. We could say they go into the collective unconscious, or into the ether, or somewhere into space. Any of these expressions would be right, for they are all ways to explain this strange phenomenon. Wherever they go, it is certain that when one vibration meets another of its own type, a unifying process occurs. One attracts another of its own type to itself. There are times when we feel angry about something, so we collect other anger out of space. If I am angry with my friend, my friend will not react to me if anger is not in him. It is the same as if I put one tuning fork at one end of the room and a second at the other end. If the second tuning fork was of the same pitch as the first, it would vibrate in sympathy when the first was struck. But, if it was of a different pitch, it would not. If someone is angry with me and I do not have anger in me, or if I am free of that type of conditioning or emotion, I will not react or feel it in myself. I will not feel anger in my own system and will not attract it to me.

Where do these vibrations go, and how do we attract them? The key here is the understanding of the nature of the psychic centers in the body, which are parts of the subtle body of man. The centers act as filter points, with the ability to transmute the energies of the invisible world so that they can be acceptable here, in this world. Once we have learned to break down the vibrations from which we are continuously becoming in our conditioned state, we can slowly but surely rebuild the body with a different type of vibration. This is the alternative. We can learn to rebuild the body with a different type of vibration, a higher form of thought, love, and aspiration, rather than being subjected to the lower vibrations in which we now live. We can cease to react like animals and learn to live on a different scale altogether.

In order to live this different way of life, it is essential to understand the enemy first. If we do not understand the nature of the conditioned mind, and if we are not truly horrified by this picture, it is very unlikely that we will work towards another way of life. The nature of the work has always been to create a new way of life by changing oneself through the work. This means changing the rate of our vibration, changing our way of thought, changing our way of reacting to circumstances. It means rising above the denseness of the Earth's structures, rising above the low vibrations of animal man, and knowing how to ascend into different planes of being—which are really planes of vibration.

The work involves realizing that "the observer" which becomes our compass if life is not, in fact, separate from us, but is our own nature. We can come to understand that the observer is our true self, and that which was trying to follow the true self was, in fact, the conditioned mind. As long as we live from the relative world, we are in duality. There is always the observer and he who is observed. If we can give ourselves up into a more absolute state, we will discover that there is less and less of a split between the observer and the observed. We will inevitably move into the alchemical marriage between Heaven and Earth, between the past and the future, between him who observes and that which is observed. When this occurs, the time delay between the planning of an experience and the experience itself exists no longer. Thought and action become one. There is even less division in space than we originally conceived there to be. The whole vibration of our life changes. No longer do we see things outside ourselves, but rather we realize that our true self contains all things.

If we are continuously becoming from these vibrations, thoughts, and emotions that never die, how is it possible to be free? If the group unconscious is with us all the time, and we can pick up the negative vibrations or the problems of the world, how can we be free? Certainly, if we raise ourselves above the dust of the relative world, we will be able to see the dust. We are still, in a sense, part of the dust, but it will not get in our nose and won't clog our vision or other senses. Without trying to escape them, we must learn to rise above those areas of the collective unconscious which influence our lives so much.

The natural heritage of the soul is pure freedom. But what is freedom? People think that freedom is getting loose from something, or getting into something else. Freedom is not these things. We will know that we are free the moment we can surrender totally to allow the free flow of life itself.

When we know who we are, we are what is, in the eternal ever-changing moment. Fear is based on the past, trying to hold onto something which is a concept of the mind. But freedom is before mind. True mind comes out of freedom. This does not mean "your" freedom or "my" freedom alone, because freedom is the flow of all that is. Freedom is expressed by the interchange of energies passing through all the king-doms of God. In the mineral world, the plant world, and the animal world, there is a flow which continues in man himself. Mind is given to man as a gift borne on the tide of freedom, but man has become enslaved by the mind itself. He has not tasted of true freedom because he is overcome by the tryanny of the stuff of mind. Electrical impulses burst upon his consciousness and make him forget his true identity. Mind is a gift which can help us to apply the knowledge of freedom, the knowledge of who and what we are. Mind is a gift of God, as the body and feelings are a gift of God. The whole elemental world is a gift which is given to the man who has come to know himself.

No teacher can bring us to freedom. No system can teach us how to be free. The teacher and the system are concepts of the truth which can lead us to the edge of the cliff. Then we are alone, frightened, wondering what would actually happen if we were to dare to jump off, to go beyond the barriers of the mind, into that pure flow of the living life that is there for all men. What we really are is within that perfect freedom, beyond mind—the source of mind. A new man may be born, whose heritage is that perfect creative freedom, who will be eternal in the knowledge of eternity itself. That is the true freedom.

The attitude of freedom is to continually surrender more and more of ourselves beyond the mind, beyond concepts, beyond all that we think we are, so that we can gradually open and awaken to the stream of life which pulses through all things. May we be awake to the all-pervading life in space, which is pure flow, without the tyranny of time. Real freedom is outside of time, where the eternal potentiality flows into and out of manifestation, immeasurable by clocks and calendars. Freedom is always here, within us. It is the natural state of the soul. What we are, it is, and what it is, we are.

The mind is a cheap thing compared to what we really are. And yet it is also a vehicle, just as our emotions are a vehicle, and as our bodies are a vehicle. The mind can be useful, but if you try to listen to what I am saying with the mind alone, you will go immediately into the world of comparison. You cannot help it. Part of you will say, "I like this," and part of you will say, "I do not like this." It is the endless swing of the grinding clash of opposites. Mind by itself will not understand. Equally well, words by themselves, without intention, are cheap things, not used correctly and not fulfilling their possible use.

The mind has another trick that is important to look at. The mind cannot accept change. It simply cannot accept change. The mind holds on, because it cannot understand change. Someone once said of meditation, that it drowns mind in love, burns mind in love. By itself, mind is a weapon against us. Mind, understood and consciously used, becomes an instrument for God's work.

Have we got the permanent I, which can observe the mind, which can make use of the mind, the emotions, the feelings, the body, but not be used by them? Have we got this thing called the permanent I? Or have we even begun to consider it?

If we are going to proceed, we need knowledge. This means, of course, the knowledge of oneself. They say that if we have knowledge of ourselves, we have everything we will ever need. It isn't enough to shoot for the stars. Towards the ordinary would be the better expression. It is better to shoot for the Earth. When a man knows the truth, he knows that this world is the resurrection.

We are here to be stewards of our planet. We are not much use if we are scattered all over the place. We have to somehow control our habits and come through the death of what we thought we were into life. Then knowledge is given.

We have to make sacrifices every minute, every hour of the day. If we build in the observer, we see the sacrifices necessary in the moment. Remember that the mind cannot understand change. The mind sees only the apparency of change. Surely we wish to come upon real change, the real change that is necessary in our time. Sacrifice is a big word. It is probably that which we want the least of anything.

It is possible to go beyond concepts, beyond the mind, and finally beyond consciousness itself. This is why climbing the ladder of sacrifice is necessary. With every step in sacrifice, there is the possibility of beginning to understand the true nature of healing. Healing means "towards wholeness." If we have a teacher or somebody around who can kick us hard enough, we will be reminded every day that sacrifice becomes an illusion if we do it for ourselves. If we make a sacrifice for ourselves alone, we will end up spiritualizing the ego and not spiritualizing the heart.

So, what is it that we can do in sacrifice? Why should we even do it, if it is not for ourselves? Can we plant a garden for the next 200 years—not for ourselves, but for the generations to come? It is hard for the mind to hold onto the realization of the necessity of sacrifice, even sacrifice for our children. The only real sacrifice is when we ask nothing in return. Anything we ask in return is an illusion; it is still a concept, which is garbage.

Just when we are beginning to understand, we come upon some interesting device or concept that might possibly lead us out of the pain we are in. We hold on to what I call the ultimate garbage, which is our concept of God. At that point, there is the greatest danger of all. Man can reach a state from which he cannot escape. It is posssible at that stage to be like a fly in a honeypot, and literally be unable to get out. We can be trapped by our concept about God and the sense that in some way we consider we know something and others do not, or that we have some special secret that takes us to what we think is God.

How many times have we done this in our relationships? We have had a concept of what the other person was, or what we wanted them to be, then took a great breath and surrendered to the concept. Then we wondered why we were so unhappy. That is not love, but is a subtle projection of the mind. If we want to come into the realization of God, we cannot limit Him by projecting a concept of Him and then surrendering to it.

If we do not earnestly desire to find God, we will not. We cannot expect Him to come to us. "If you take one step toward God, He takes ten toward you." We have to make the first step. We need to seek that we may find. We need to know that the door is always open.

In this moment, life is the only teacher. We can only be pupils of life, and awaken to our place in the scheme of things. Methods emerge which may push us to the edge, to the brink of comprehension. They cannot deliver us to the waters of life. Only men and women, themselves, can take that plunge. All the systems, all the forms of religion have been tremendously useful in the past, bringing us to the point of surrendering all that we think we are. And then, at last, we are able to discover the nature of who and what we are. We are brought to realization of self.

T HE SEARCH FOR IDENTITY *"We can make that great surrender of all that we think we are, to discover, at last, the nature of who and what we are."*

What then is man? This search for identity at the core of our existence creates a paradox. Initially, we are led away from ourselves through everything else. Then, ultimately, we are guided back to our true selves again, in recognition of our true nature as a particular mode of the One who is the unchanging essence of all. The discovery of our essential selves is a result of the continual dying to the world of illusion. Only that which is essential remains alive. Arriving at this point of knowledge is only possible through conscious suffering and the sacrifice of the illusions we hold about ourselves. This requires an unconditional surrender to a life of service to God and humanity.

Man has a very special place in the universal picture. It has been said, "What a plant does unconsciously a person needs to do consciously." In the scale of being, man has the choice of remaining in an unconscious state to perform the functions of an animal, or he can bring himself to an awareness of natural law. Eventually he can take part in the direction of an impulse in accord with this law. At the top of the scale there is just one law; there is one absolute Being. But at a certain point the law can fulfill itself on Earth only through the agreement of man. It is our obligation in being man to say, "Oh Lord, let Thy Will be done, not mine." This is the key to the path of service and surrender. Without man who is conscious of the law and of his place in the scale of being, no more than a pale shadow of the perfection and glory of the law can be manifested on Earth.

When we look at the planet today, it is obvious how man's lack of understanding, coupled with his greed and ignorance, has managed to make him not the husbandman of the Earth, as Adam was asked to be, but rather the rapist of the planet itself. The Earth is the Mother, the woman who carries the seed in her womb as it grows back toward the light. We have stolen from the Mother, who, uncomplaining, has borne the pillage of the past and is only now showing us the results of our stupidity. Now man must understand woman, and the creative female energy, so that he may learn to catalyze the Earth's energy with cosmic force to give birth to a golden age—the second cycle of mankind.

I am convinced that mankind now has to put itself wholeheartedly on the path of service. With this must come the understanding of female energy. To try to enter the path of service without the balance of masculine and feminine energies, yin and yang, in harmony will lead to disharmony in the end, even if on the surface the disharmony may not be immediately obvious. So far, the Western world has been dominated by the male force. The West is now turning toward the female force as the East picks up the role of male force in the world. This works in the same way as the hemispheres of the brain, which take turns being dominant in our lives. We must be careful not to turn the woman's role into that which was formerly filled by the man. What is needed now is a change of attitude toward female energy, not a reversal of roles.

Yet I am not referring here to the outer form of the balance of man and woman, but to the underlying energies that exist equally in both man and woman, Heaven and Earth. Whatever is seen in the outer world is a result of that which exists on the inner planes of endless, interpenetrating, vibrating worlds of light. Too long have we in the West looked only to the dominant male force. This has created great technological advances while being blind and destructive to the needs of the female, the Earth itself, this beautiful planet we call home.

Perhaps we have lost the capacity to listen and to be receptive. We now must learn to balance our actions with passion. We must now learn, if we are to survive at all, to listen to the needs of the Earth, in the understanding that if we do listen, the answer can be given as to what should be done. From the true alchemical marriage, which has never yet been consummated, will come the second birth, the golden age, or second cycle of mankind. And mankind itself is the catalyst that will bring about the necessary transformation.

To come to the first stage of realization, we must come to know the life force, to begin to serve within and for a group, and to learn to live detached within the body. To know our true identity, we must know the vehicle we are given, and the life force, the Mother. Then we may begin to work in cooperation with the three worlds, which is only possible when we are awake to who we are.

Man has a threefold nature. The three worlds are represented within him as a microcosm, and only in man is this correspondence manifested. There are three centers to the activities of man, through which man may function if he is truly conscious of his being: the moving center, the feeling center, and the thinking center. These centers seldom function in harmony with one another due to the aberrant psyche of ordinary man. One center is always over- or under-stimulated in relation to another, and different types of men may be classified according to which center they depend upon most in their activities.

Another way to examine the tripartite nature of man is to refer to three of the subtle bodies of man: the etheric body, which has to do with sensations (not senses); the astral body, which has to do with feelings; and the mental or causal body, which has to do with objective reason. The etheric light web encloses that which makes up the physical body, composed of the four elements of fire, air, earth, and water. The etheric substance can be seen as an intricate web through which energy is taken via the various subtle centers to energize the physical body. The astral body links us to the astral plane and charges the physical body with feelings. The mental body links us to the causal plane via ideas, not ordinary thoughts, and connects the person to the source of objective reason and knowledge.

We all know that the physical form responds or reacts to sensations, thoughts, and feelings, and that it does not cause these sources of its reactions. But the way to freedom lies in realization that the essential self is more central than any thought, feeling, or sensation can ever be. Let us bless the three bodies and cleanse them with light, giving thanks that we have them to use, but realizing that we are not identical with these bodies.

If we are not our thoughts, or our feelings, or our sensations, who or what are we? "Seek ye first the Kingdom of God" means we should turn within and detach ourselves from our identification with the sheaths that contain us. By slowly dissolving any conception of what we think or feel or sense we are, we can come to that wonderful moment when we can be sure of our own identity. Then we can affirm the one absolute Existence from which all life springs. "Be still and know that I am God within you."

Now, if man does have a special place in the cosmic order, then there must also be the knowledge of how he can fulfill his mission. In the absolute sense, every being is a part of the work of transmutation. It is usually only through death that a sufficient amount of energy is released to be of any benefit to the work. There are some people who have special gifts which can be developed to assist consciously in the workings of this law. But to do this we must understand that there is but one Being in existence. We then must find the law at work and train ourselves to be strong and adaptable enough to assist in the unfolding of this law.

THE PATH OF RETURN *"Man is the mediator between the One and the Many."*

When man surrenders all that he thinks he is, including his concept of what ought to be done to be in touch with the cause of all creation, the little "I"—his concept of identity—is melted, little by little. He is placed in the stream of manifestation from the invisible to the visible, from Being to becoming.

As he gives of himself, so he is given back the tools he will need to help the great plan. He is given what he needs, which is what God needs, to fulfill His work on Earth.

The other aspect of this principle has been called "the path of return." Many years ago, it was such a wonderful feeling for me to know that I was entering a path which would return me to God. At that time I had no idea of the true nature of self. It seemed that the "me" that was searching would return into the arms of the Beloved. I would be one with Him and that would be it. In simple terms this is exactly what does happen. No one can tell us who we are; but when we come upon that knowledge, the "path of return" brings about a sense of responsibility that previously had been veiled by the illusionary self. It is then that we are offered the choice either to become immersed in the totality of all life, or, in taking upon ourselves the name of man, to assist consciously in the workings of God's law.

The law of reciprocal maintenance of the planet has two sides to it. These involve the cyclic manifestation of a principle, the way up and the way down, evolution and involution. In the first instance, man sacrifices all that he thinks he is in prayer and in the act of total surrender to God's Will. In the second, he acts as the channel through which that Will can be made manifest on Earth. What is it that he is sacrificing in his prayer, or rather, what is it that is returning through man's prayer? Is it through the sacrifice of man's personal will that all of God's creatures return to God? Could it be that only through man is all life allowed to take the path of return? We know that it cannot be a one-way process.

Oneness is not the miracle. The miracle is that there can be "the many" or "everything," which is appearing within "the One" or "the All." Just as "the many" are longing to manifest themselves, so also the many, once manifested, seek reunion with the One or the All. Man is the mediator between the One and the many. As such, he acts as a valve, which allows things into creation by saying "I will," and which also allows them to reunite with the One. Man is to God as the pupil is to the eye. It is through man, perfected man, that God beholds his creatures, has mercy upon them, and fills them with being.

The key to man's role in assisting the path of return came to me in this sentence: "Please remember, they do not know that you can recognize them." This means that all of God's creatures do not know that He can see them, know them, and give them being through man's recognition of them. But what is it that man can recognize in other creatures? The recognition is not just the outward form, the visible aspects, but the inner qualities present in the creature. A tree does not know that we can recognize its value, nor does a fish, animal, or bird. Do the various invisible beings that make up our own body, emotions, and mind, know that we can recognize them? The many feel isolated and separated from their source. They struggle with each other for life or ignore each other. Think of the endless battles and personality struggles that are entailed in human relationships because of the lack of recognition of the inner values of other people. How wonderful it would be if we could cultivate the quality of recognition of the oneness of all life. It is only through the awakening of the dormant aspects of the oneness that we can resolve the pain and anguish felt by the many in their illusion of separation and feeling of rejection. The many are like the Sleeping Princess, who longs to be awakened by the "kiss" of man, the Prince, so that the path of return may be traveled. When there is a true light within a man, all creatures will come to him, like moths to the flame. It is only through the light of knowledge of the One that the creatures can return to their Source and true home.

Once during a talk I was giving, a huge orange butterfly came and landed on my left hand. There was a great surge of love in the group, and we said "Thank you," to the One for granting us this sign. The butterfly then flew around the group and came back and landed on my knee. A third time it came, as though in great joy, and in front of all of us, spiraled its way upwards until we lost sight of it over the Hudson River. A little later, in Aspen, Colorado, while visiting a friend there, I was explaining the same concept. Suddenly we were surrounded with birds who seemed to come down out of the trees to participate in that great moment as we came into the realization of the kingdoms. Then little animals came out of the rocks, and we stood there, glorifying and praising the wonder of God's worlds, the insubstantial, shimmering essence of all life that pervades and permeates everything. The key is in the word recognition—the recognition that we always were one with the Divine, but over the eons we have forgotten and therefore need to work to remember once again who we were, are, and will be evermore. Our responsibility is to train that which lies within us to respond to that recognition.

Man has forgotten his responsibility to the life force, the female energy. He has put to sleep the "mind of matter" and kept it away from the path of return. Only now is he beginning to see the result of his forgetfulness, as the Earth has been brought to the point of death. The imbalance of energies, if man could only see it, necessitates an urgency to the work that must be done to save the planet. If man can awaken to his true identity, he will know himself as the Prince, and remember the sleeping Princess, perhaps in time to embrace her back to life along the path of return.

The world of nature is a force to be reckoned with, because it has been blocked by man's forgetfulness of his responsibility. Because man has forgotten his identity, he does not perform his work of reciprocal maintenance. The forces of the elemental world are trying to return in whatever way they can, even if it means taking over a human body to do so. Yet if man can reawaken to the responsibility inherent in his position, then it is possible to enlist the aid of the elemental world. They long to go home! They long to cooperate in the great plan, if only man will let them.

What we need now is an understanding of what we might call conscious love. Love is the motivating force of all creation. It is the strongest and most fundamental force in the universe. We need to be able to consciously anchor and apply the force of love, which is only possible if we know who and what we are. We must find that place in ourselves, called the soul, which is the substance which knows of our essential identity with the one Source.

Love, which is absolute, splits into two aspects the moment the word "I" is spoken. "The One divides in order to unite," and this division is the secret of the trinity. The One divides to make the two, which immediately creates the three; it takes three forces to manifest anything. From the threeness springs forth the myriad of beings that exist within the body of God. This is the Kingdom of God. The responsibility of man is to know the meaning of the One, or the word "I." It is in this knowledge that he moves away from his role as an animal to gain the immortal heritage of the soul, which is perfect freedom and knowledge of the essential self.

We have forgotten the responsibility which comes with saying the word "I." If we would only awaken to the truth of our being, which cannot be understood with the mind as we know it, we would learn to be more careful and aware when we say, "I love you." When we say these words, we bring into play a force that was not there before, a force that has its own job to do regardless of ours. This force is the invisible kingdom which carries on its work on the elemental scale until man turns. It is only in the act of saying "I" that the path of return is opened.

It is not difficult to see the working of this force in our everyday life, which is controlled, for the most part, by "our" desires. We consider the actions of the elemental force to be "our" thoughts, "our" feelings, and "our" choices. We believe that, somehow, we have created them. Our lives run through a series of habit patterns that we seem unable to break. We produce various symptoms of illness that are manifested in various ways. Nearly always they stem from the same source, which is the lack of a true identity that can take responsibility for saying "I." As long as we do not know who we are, we are led along blindly by the forces of destiny. We are imprisoned in a form of false gravity, perhaps to awaken at the very end of our life to see that, in fact, we have done nothing.

The way out of the dilemma of being at the mercy of the elemental world is to enter the path of service. We all know that when we work for the welfare of another, think of another, put ourselves last, a different thing happens. There is a sense of liberation and a freedom from the tyranny of thoughts and self-centered feelings. When we are open to the path of service, we are immediately filled with light and freed from the cocoon of habits which veil our essential selves. When we begin to understand the law of service, we begin to be born. It requires constant work and reaffirmation of our willingness, if we are to be freed permanently from the habit patterns which have prevented our real lives. If we dedicate our lives to work in the way of service, not for our own benefit, we will be directly helped by beings of a different order altogether, whose job it is to see that reciprocal mainte- nance of the planet is fulfilled. But it is only when man says "I will" in consciousness that the cooperation of these forces is possible as an act of love.

We find that what is called a "dome" separating higher man from lower man. We can find the interval that is called the dome in man in the area between the solar plexus and the heart. This is a point of tension, or tightening, which acts to stop the flow of energy through man from Heaven to Earth and back again. The relaxation of the filter, which is the dome, is an important part of the work that a man must do to free himself for participation in the divine plan. This plan can only act through him according to the degree to which his resistances have been melted.

The first stage in this process, called "coming into being," occurs when we first cross the threshold, through work on ourselves, to move our center of gravity from the solar plexus to the heart center. If this process is correctly accomplished, with all the centers in balance, we enter a state of being in which the impartial observer can become aware of the work- ings of natural law. This awareness will release a certain type of energy into the brain and nervous system, which awakens in us dormant faculties beyond the normal six senses (intellect being considered as a faculty or sense). This springing into life is called insight or revelation. It accompanies the opening of the heart in conscious love and service.

The opening of the heart can occur only when we have worked on the self long enough to be freed from the illusory dominance of our animal nature. In this process, the geometry of habitual patterns becomes liquid, so that there is an upward flow of return within us.

We can see why the alchemical marriage of Heaven and Earth must take place in the heart of man. Only a small amount of the life energy can flow back to the source until we ourselves change. If we see this, then we can welcome the shocks that are given to melt us and to send us through the eye of the needle. We will learn to recognize that the intentional suffering we undergo is necessary for the evolutionary process of the planet itself.

There is an old saying, "Hell hath no fury like a woman scorned." Indeed, there is no fury greater than the unadulterated life force which wishes to return, but is thwarted again and again by the forgetfulness of man. What do we understand of the consciousness of our own planet at this moment?

All prayer begins with praise, and it is prayer that spirals evolution. True evolution begins and ends in praise of the beauty of God's creation and in heartfelt gratitude that we are able to participate consciously in His works. With the realization that man is the manifested consciousness of God, we realize the unity in diversity and the joy of working in our different ways in cooperation with God's plan. We are breaking through into uncharted horizons. There is a new world ahead, a golden age coming out of darkness. It is only through perfected man that the law can be made manifest. "I was a hidden treasure and I longed to be known, so I created the world that I might be known." (hadith of the Prophet Mohammed, may the peace and blessings of God be upon him). His purpose in the first place was that He could know Himself once more through His servant, mankind.

THE NEED FOR WILL *"Let us develop will, that we can truly be of service."*

When we learn love, we shall have will. Will is the beginning of the first step on a long journey from beliefs to knowledge. Mastery of our own will is the door that leads to service. When we can choose to allow God's Will to be done in us, we are in service.

If we have will, then we can use our will to let go and be a vehicle for God's use. We can be driven (like a car) from the inside, instead of being pushed and towed around by outward appearances.

Will is the ability to fulfill responsibility and obligation; that is, to know responsibility and act accordingly. It is the ability not to waste time wondering and thinking about what responsibility is or should be, but to know on all inner levels. Having will allows the inner voice of authority to be heard, thereby freeing us from the chaotic dissonance of outward authority or social pressure.

An important factor in learning to have will, at least for me, has been the understanding and perception that I am loved. In the knowledge that in essence I am loved lies a key to unlock me from the chains of my self pity, which endlessly ensnare me in "poor me, nobody loves me and I can't do anything." When I know this love, I know that there is a reason for my suffering. It is as if I were a balloon floating, and the pain that I feel is a string that pulls me back from the "reality" that has been an illusion of reality. It reminds me that there is more than my small needs, which most of the time I refuse to let go of. For me, the knowledge of love is the beginning of will.

Will is the beginning of the becoming of Being.

Why is it that so many people cringe at the mention of the word "will" and are afraid even to think about it? Why is it that so many people on the path towards realization still do not understand the gifts of God? Will is a gift, as are all the other attributes that lie in waiting within man. Because we think we already have "will," we do not call upon what is really a potential for the having of will. If we do not know who we are, then we cannot say that we have will. People are afraid of being too self-willed. They pray saying, "Let Thy Will be done, not mine," thinking that they have no responsibility in the process. But if we remember that there is one absolute Being, we will realize that all creation is an expression of an Infinite Will.

Now is the time when humanity needs to awaken and develop its will. Each individual is a unique example of the one Being and has the responsibility of bringing forth the latent qualities and attributes established in his soul. If each man develops his will, he is fulfilling the intention of bringing forth the Will of God on Earth. It is in humanity that the Will of God is most free. God has free-will in man, whenever man says "I will."

To develop will requires a lot of work. First, there has to be the intention to develop will, and much work must be done to clear the character defects in ourselves, which serve to confuse the intention that has already been given to each one of us. Once we come to understand the unity of all life, our intentions take on a different quality. In ordinary life we make a vague intention to complete some task or other, to clean the floor, wash the dishes, make a living, or write a book, but all these intentions are based upon what we have known in the past and what we expect in the future. We make our intentions based on the past, conditioned by the illusion of false time.

A real intention is made outside of time. Herein lies a great riddle. If we are a part of this world, we are made up of the stuff of time; how can we make an intention outside of time? The answer is so simple that the mind cannot possibly understand it! The mind wants to analyze it, compute it, complicate it, plan it, and explain it, but the real intention needs no explanation, nor *can* it be explained.

The Sufis say that the true dervish is not necessarily responsible for his actions. This may seem to deny the ordinary understanding of the purpose of the spiritual path, but if we consider the state of an intention made outside of time, we can recognize that we are not the judge of how the intention is going to be manifested. God knows best. He is the Judge, not we. A true dervish, then, cannot be responsible for his actions, but he is responsible for his intentions. Action is in life, within time, and subject to the laws of the world. The dervish sets his intention outside of time and then surrenders his will so that the intention can be actualized through him. Until the world is free, there will continue to be a great many influences that will interfere with the manifestation of the intention. Like a leaf caught in the autumn wind, the intention is taken hither and yon, so that no one can predict exactly where and how it will land. The dervish knows that the leaf will go where it should.

The leaf may land on the lap of an old man in the park, or surprise a dog, or tickle the nose of a couple kissing on the beach. It may be blown into a dirty street corner, to bring a little color to the dirty concrete. It may be swirled into a spiral to join other leaves. It might be collected by a man to make compost, which will help to grow and maintain the glory of God's Kingdom. It might flutter down from the tree alone and dissolve into humus.

The dervish is both here and not here. His intention to be one with God is made outside time, unconditionally. He recognizes his unity with the life which pervades and permeates all things. His every heartbeat is an action of the pulse of life itself. With his heartbeat, leaves burst into the universe, waves crash upon the sea, the seasons rotate, the cosmic dance of the stars revolves, the Earth turns. He stands as the thread between Heaven and Earth, at the still point of the turning world, at the intersection of time and the timeless, where the dance is.

At this point of turning, we join the dervish in the true attitude of will. In knowledge of the unity of the one Will, the dervish expresses the willingness to participate consciously in the harmonious unfolding of the three worlds. This unfolding can only come about through the agreement of man. God's Will, man's will. When man makes the intention to serve God unconditionally, this intention is beyond the limits of time.

This is the perfect man; this is the man who has come to know and love God so perfectly that his every action is an expression of the Will of God.

The exercise of intention acts as a bridge between the eternal and the temporal. This bridge is the true nature of man. The bridge is so frail that we need to be in a perfect state of awareness before a crossing can be made. Beneath the bridge is a roaring torrent which would sweep us away into unconsciousness. At this stage we have to be absolutely clear about our decision to incarnate God's will and involve ourselves in life. This is the point of giving up our will into the Will of God, the point Jesus came to in the Garden of Gethsemane. This is the stage where a vow is taken, the vow that we will continue to work in the world to help others to be free.

DECISION *"The major way to conquer fear is to make a decision."*

Danger is everywhere. Since the fall from grace, there has always been the ultimate temptation. Every single step that we take brings about some sort of danger. We cannot avoid this. If we pick up one foot, for a brief moment we have only one leg to stand on, and so there is danger. If we take our eyes off the truth for a split second of time, then that which stands against truth—for it knows not better!—is there in the breach.

We should not avoid danger; but neither should we tempt fate. If we do, one day it will overtake us. The reason for this may not be apparent at first glance, but it is simple. You see, fate is an aspect of the totality that demands to be recognized in a very special way. It cannot know, in itself, that it is recognized. Yet, deep inside, there is something which does know, but which has forgotten or will not accept.

Fate is like a great tidal wave. If left to its own time it will finally calm down and things will be all right once again. But it would be suicidal to try to surf-ride a tidal wave! It would be foolish indeed, and yet that is what we frequently do. We tempt fate in the way that we drive our cars, in the way we approach our responsibilities to life, in the way we treat the environment, the Earth that gives us sustenance. We have tempted fate long enough! At the rate things are going it will not be long before fate takes charge. The Earth will speak with a voice that is louder than any words.

Yet we must not avoid danger. What does this mean? Danger automatically comes about as the result of the decision-making process. It is not possible to make a real decision without involving danger. We cannot even make a decision to go out for dinner, taking the family and a few friends and perhaps driving ten miles to some favorite restaurant, without there being danger. It is simply not possible. The average sleeping man does not see this, and if he has a car crash, or if the food is dreadful, or if the child burns his fingers in the soup, or if the battery of the car goes dead while he and his friends are having dinner, he blames the situation. He even blames inanimate objects, as if there could be blame on an inanimate object! Blame is placed everywhere but within. He has refused to accept the danger of any decision. For any decision precipitating any action carries with it untold danger.

We are not to be negative about this. Let us look at the implications. We are not mineral, nor are we vegetable, and one day, all being well (!), we will not be animal. So what on earth are we? We have instincts, feelings, and emotions, but we are not these. If we are not these things, then again what are we, and what could be our purpose on Earth? If our true destiny is to become conscious human beings, *hu-manas,* meaning *Hu* (God) and *manas* (mind), or God-conscious creatures, then, by the very implication of the words, we are not only able to make decisions on our own, but also we are able to know what the decision should be, and the potential results. We are able to have joy, to live joyfully—a state unique to man. And tell me, what greater joy is there than that which comes out of making a conscious decision?

Joy is not what we call happiness. Joy is the fusion of knowledge and feeling which overflows as understanding.

But knowledge necessitates decision, and decision is bound to bring danger. "A gnostic is not allowed *not* to take action."

Welcome danger, and all that it means. But have knowledge of the laws that govern danger. Have the knowledge that stems from deeds of self-denial and true acts of service in our lives. Then we will have all the "helpers" along the way to see us through the danger.

Danger, like creative tension, is necessary in the same way as internal friction, which increases the heat of the fire. Danger opens us. "The One divides in order to unite." Division is given to us that there may be a mirror through which we can see ourselves, through which He can see Himself in us, through which He knows Himself, and we know ourselves in Him. Thus there is only Him.

Danger lurks at every corner when one makes a decision to undergo real change and not the apparency of change.

"How does one conquer fear?"

The major way to conquer fear is to make a decision. If we fight fear without a decision, it gets worse. Fear is an illusion. On the lowest level, the mind starts rattling from one thing to the other, trying to grab hold. The mind is always trying to grab hold of something, and because it cannot, we feel fear. Within the mind there technically are fourteen steps. It really does not matter how they work, but there is one dimensionless point of energy from which the mind spreads out like a great dome. Its only limitation occurs when we say "my mind" or "your mind." Because the first law in the esoteric path is "energy follows thought," the moment we say "my mind," energy follows that thought. It is like shining a bit of energy on one point of the mind and saying this is what the mind is. Unfortunately, it does not work like that because the other portion of the mind is saying, "No, I am over here. I am over there. I am behind." As a result, we have this state that exists inside us which we call "fear." Fear has a seat in the human body, like any other so-called negative emotion. Fear is seated in the solar plexus.

Suppose for instance, something had once happened to you on a particular road somewhere and you later drove along that road. If the memory pattern was still there, you would be frightened at the same place that the previous instance occurred. The fear would come up again. If, on the other hand, you had made a conscious decision to travel from here to there on that portion of the road, you might have a certain twinge, but you would just go through it.

Decision is the first way of conquering fear. We need to be working on how to use will in everyday life, for good. Every time we are in a state of fear, as opposed to being in awe of God, we are lost, asleep. The moment we are in fear we go to sleep. All of us suffer from this in varying degrees, because we are all human beings.

We must not be frightened or ashamed of fear either, because every time we are ashamed of fear, we have more fear. Let us say that there is a forest fire and all of us here have to go and fight it. It does not mean to say there is not fear, but the fear does not stop us from fighting the fire. There is something to do, a real thing to do. We get out and do it, and sooner or later by making that decision we conquer fear.

We start with the simplest possible thing: "What is there to do? When am I going to do it? How am I going to do it?" The danger of making a decision—however small—and not fulfilling it is acute. That is why these things are normally given to people who have worked for some time. If we make a decision and we do not fulfill it, then we have an inner shame. The mind, which is energy, wants to be given something to do. If the mind has nothing to do, it runs amuck. The effect in us is shame, and that occurs in the area of self pity. The result is fear that I cannot do it any more, fear I cannot do anything. That is because we have not fulfilled what we said we were going to do.

Making a conscious decision every day is something we can work on, and then eventually the fear will start to go. None of us are perfect; only God is perfect. We always have some secret little something or other hidden which makes us go on looking. If we did not have something wrong, we would not go on looking. He requires us to go on looking. He likes to hear our prayers. The highest level of prayer is the state of knowledge. Only when there is total knowledge of God can there be no fear. It is said that fear of the Lord is the beginning of wisdom, yet "He who knows himself, knows his Lord." The highest level is the knowledge of God. The more we study and the more we work to know Him, the less fear there is.

Every decision produces some degree of creative tension. It is within that creative tension that grace may enter. If we allow ourselves to be used and worked by fate, then there is no creative tension. Fate takes us over and we either feel "good" or "not good." It may seem that this clash of opposite states produces the necessary tension, but this is not so. It is merely lower work to do with the emotional body.

Creative tension is not like this. It comes from making a conscious decision, and that decision is irrevocable. We cannot go back on a decision we make consciously. If we do, we lose will. Will and Spirit go together and without these we are nothing. We are merely animals playing the game of being human. It is rather like a dog who lives very close to its master, longing to serve, longing to be recognized, but which is only useful to fulfill the task given to it, whether it be as a protector or an ally.

Thus, I ask everyone to make a conscious decision every day, without fail. It is up to us. No one can do it for us. We can be given the methods, and thus a way to live for the future of our children and mankind as a whole, but no one, I repeat, no one can do it for us.

D EVELOPING WILL *"Without will we are likely to repeat habit patterns of the past again and again."*

If we have no will, how can we develop will?

Once it is seen that we have no will, we tend to feel totally miserable because we cannot do anything. Let us see what "doing" means. What actually activates any movement is mere habit. We can say we eat a meal when we feel hungry, and then we wash the dishes. Very rarely do we make a conscious decision to sit down at a table, eat, get up, and then do the dishes. We just do it as a normal habit pattern. We think we are actually doing something. Our jaws move up and down; food goes in; there is some kind of digestive process; and we keep going.

Let us say that we are, by profession, architects. Obviously architects take "out of the blue," out of the visionary world, the possibility of constructing a great house or building of some sort. Doing something implies bringing order into the world. There are a great many architects who plunk down houses with no relationship to any other house. This is not really doing anything creative. The houses are often put next to each other, but they have no relationship whatsoever. The buildings may be creative, but nothing is really being done. They have only served to feed someone's ego. We can take any profession as an example. Something appears to be done but nothing really is being done. Doing implies bringing order out of chaos. The answer very simply is—Be awake to order.

There comes a crucial point in life when we wish to help bring about order into a waiting world. For this to be fulfilled we need to realize that we have no will. Until we can complete the most simple thing, such as a decision, where is will?

There is a very great danger of getting into a negative state because "we have no will." There are two attitudes. The first is the attitude that "I have something coming up and I must work through it." The second is concerned with "the way I was raised or the way I raise my own children." As far as I am concerned, when something is coming up, one does best to get on with it. It will come up and go. The moment one starts thinking about it, it gets worse. People in that state should be given a paint brush and told to paint something. Do not think about negativity. It can go on for years and years. The answer is to get on and stop complaining. If we wail that it is not possible to see the mountains, God's beauty, or anything, then it *is* not possible and we never see what there is to be done. If we have will, we see what there is to be done and get on with it. If we are wailing, we are drawing attention to our illusions.

We do not have to worry about what is coming up or going out if we truly give ourselves to this work which is called a life of service.

Will has to do with fulfilling something. I have always wondered why people do not want to develop will. I can say that we can reach a point whereby if we fail our responsibility as human beings, the will that is needed on Earth may no longer be possible. Eventually, we can lose so much of a certain type of subtle energy that the possibililty of regaining the true possibility of our lives on Earth no longer exists. The younger we are started upon understanding the importance of will, the better. If we can get people to see the meaning of the possibility of will before they are seven years old, they will not revert to a fixed pattern set up by the initial shock that usually stops their development. It is especially in the first seven years, and then the second seven years, that we can work with children to see the rewards of will.

How do we will to have will? The way to have will is to want it. Why do we want it? We want to help build a better world. Without will we could repeat habit patterns of the past again and again. Will to be awake to order. Will to be of service. If we are asleep, it is not possible to be of service.

If we honestly stop for a moment to look at the way we have lived our lives, we will discover that most of the time we have lived a continuous battle. This battle in our inner lives is expressed in the outer world as a struggle to fulfill some task. To give a very simple analogy: consider someone at the office, normally with an immense amount of work to do. At the end of the day, he is confronted with what he set out to do in the morning and how much of it he still has left to do. An office efficiently run works only if what is agreed to be done is completed. We can complete only as much as we have the capacity to do. If we try to do too much then the battle becomes worse. We find ourselves unable to complete all that we set out to do. Soon we have a desk piled with unattended situations. Our nerves get shattered and we do not know what to do next. At its worst, the business goes broke.

The word "humility" enters here. We need to be humble

enough to accept our own capacity and never try to do more than we can cope with at any one moment. It is the same with everything in daily life. Some people have greater capacity; some are even able to think consciously of several things at once without getting into a total muddle; others do not have the same capacity. We need to look carefully at what we really can do and then fulfill what we set out to do in the first place.

However, there is much more here that we can look at. The first thing is to realize that until we truly enter the work, and that means entering with all of our being, we rarely "do" anything consciously. Instead, we fall into situations that we have little or no control over and then wonder why, at the end of the day, we do not feel fulfilled. You see, we are fulfilled only when we make a conscious decision to do something and complete it.

"Consciousness" implies that we are conscious. To be conscious means we have to be awake, attuned to the moment and willing to fulfill whatever task we are given. If we are not willing, then we resent whatever it is that we are attempting to do. This may be a very subconscious resentment but the resentment is still there. The ultimate resentment, hidden deep within our psyche, comes about from our lack of willingness even to be here on this planet at this time. There is a further dimension to consider when we use the word "willing." As consciousness implies that we are conscious, willingness implies that we have some sort of will.

I do not wish to sound hard, but we need will in order to complete a cycle that is made consciously. Without will, we are nothing and nothing is done. If we look very honestly at our own lives, we may discover how little will we have. Unfortunately, very few teachers stress the need of will and discipline. Will and inner discipline are like two hands on one body.

We want to give God back something since He gives us everything. It is said that there are only two things we are asked to give Him in gratitude for all that He gives us: service and dependence.

Now, what do these two words actually mean? Dependence means willingly accepting our complete dependence upon Him who is the only provider, Him who is the only guide, Him who is the All-Knowing.

It is very hard to be totally willing to accept this, is it not? So often "we" feel that we somehow or other can do this or that on our own. If we forget that we are totally dependent on His eternal bounty, then what we think we "do" will be nothing more than a repetition of an illusion and a feeding of our own lower nature or egoism.

The more we feed the lower nature, the more in separation we are. The more we are in separation, the more inner pain there is. Of course, since He also provides the law and the rules therein, by not fulfilling His commands, our responsibilities, the pain of separation may get worse. If we are reminded of these matters, our yearning gets greater! However, that is no excuse not to fulfill our obligations! To be willing to realize our dependence brings us, once again, to the importance of being awake and respectful, and, indeed, conscious of the law.

Our way is a way of love, compassion and service. It is true that without being willing servants of God, we are not fulfilling our obligations in this world, and indeed in our daily lives. A gnostic is not allowed not to take action.

The word "will" has been continuously stressed. Perhaps we now realize that what is being said is that we do not have much will until we learn how to have it. Will lies within, waiting to be brought forth.

The question is, first of all, how do we develop will; secondly, how do we apply it to everyday life; and thirdly, what is the purpose of will? Within these three questions lies the answer to "What is the purpose of life on Earth?"

There are many practices that can be given to help us understand these things and also fulfill our obligation in being born onto this planet. If we are willing to learn, we will respect what we are given and fulfill our task. From being "willing," there is the possibility of developing real will within. When we have real will, we have something very real to give back to God.

So often we talk about the Will of God. Sometimes we are humble enough to ask the question, What indeed is the Will of God? Without will of our own, it is not possible to understand what the Will of God is. When we have gained will, then we may give that will to the greater Will of God, and then there is only Will. Thus there is the fulfillment of the first law of alchemy: "As above, so below." Did not Jesus say, "Thy Will be done on Earth as it is in Heaven"?

The Sufis say, "God needs man." It is through man (the perfected man who has come to know and love God perfectly) that Love, which is the motivating force behind all creation, can flow into this world. The invocation of a conscious man, "Let Thy kingdom come, Thy will be done, on earth as it is in heaven," brings into play a law, in essence perfect, seeking only to manifest itself. We can see the unfolding first appearing as a thought, which could be seen as a being. The thought wishes to manifest itself. It attaches itself to the world of feelings so that man will wish for it to be. Thus, it is charged with life and eventually proceeds into manifestation, having passed through all three worlds.

We can see the working of this law in any act of creation. Let us consider the making of a chair. If everyone were sitting around on a cold and damp stone floor, someone would eventually say, "We must have chairs." Whether they used the word or not, they would still have an idea of what was needed to keep them off the floor. This idea comes from the archetype of all those objects which have certain qualities which we may call "chairness," in this case implying an article that would have a back, seat, and legs in order to fulfill its intended function. The archetype wishes to express itself in this world, because there is a certain knowledge that it would be useful and necessary. But if the archetype of chairness remains only an idea in someone's mind, and we all continue sitting on the stone floor holding the archetypal idea of "chair," nothing has really happened. It is only when someone says "I will" to the idea and gets up to begin making a chair that anything at all happens.

Once someone has said "I will" to the making of a chair, there still remain the tasks of making drawings, gathering materials and tools, and finding the time and space to do the work, before there is a real possibility of bringing a chair into manifestation. For this process to unfold, certain conditions are necessary: a direct intention to make the chair; energy and direction sufficient to fulfill the intention; and the knowledge of the various stages of the process, which includes knowing the places where extra effort needs to be made to keep the flow of creation going.

A good servant has to have will to fulfill the function he or she has been given. Fulfillment indeed comes from the joy of knowing what it means to be a good servant.

Every woman in the world longs for every man to have will and to manifest the Spirit. Here I am not just talking about woman in the physical form but also including the Divine Mother. There is not one portion of the Earth that is not open to receive the Spirit. There is a saying, "Wheresoe'er ye stand, that is holy ground." That means standing in will, that the Spirit of God may manifest itself upon the Earth. Indeed, when we do have will, wherever we stand is holy. "Holy" means "whole," so when the Spirit of God enters the waiting world, it becomes whole and is complete.

Now we can look at the application of will in daily life as an act of service, but only if we are willing to accept the responsibility. It is hard to talk about the application of will if we do not yet have will. To "apply" means to give something that we have, to something that is already waiting to receive. The application of will in daily life is only possible when we are open to the truth that the moment is indeed waiting to receive the Spirit.

I remember when I was studying with the Druids. The Arch-Druid himself said to me, "Basically, the world is divided into two: those who feel that this is a fit place in which to live and serve, and those who do not. I belong to the former. I pray that you, too, will be one of those who will serve God by serving the planet—the home He has given us—in which and through which we can come to know Him."

Like the Druid, I will repeat the same: I pray that we will come to know Him by serving Him. He has given us this beautiful world which, when we have will, we may turn into holy ground. If we work hard enough and if we long to be good servants in the realization of our total dependence upon Him who gives all life, then we have begun to fulfill our obligation in being allowed to be born man and woman.

Let us develop will, that we can truly be of service. Let us never, for one moment, be so self-satisfied that we feel we can do anything—until we have willingly accepted the knowledge that is available to us, if we will only ask. "Seek, and ye shall find; knock, and it shall be opened unto you." Amen.

A TTUNEMENT *"It is dependent upon the quality of the note we strike as to what is given to us in return."*

There is a saying, "The whole on high hath a part in our dancing." Every time we strike a note, and I don't just mean a note on the piano, immediately, "The whole on high hath a part in our dancing." The angels, we might say, are harmonics; when a note is struck, its harmonic responds. If we take a piano and strike a note, immediately the harmonics respond. There is a saying in the Sufi tradition, "Take one step towards God, He takes ten towards you." Our responsibility in taking one step towards truth, towards God, brings about immediately all the help we will ever need. Everything we need is there; how long it takes to manifest is another matter. The moment we take that step, that turning towards God, we get all the help we need. That is why in our tradition we turn, not for ourselves, but for the world; why we meditate, not for ourselves, but for the world.

From the beginning of time, man has attempted to attune himself to the formative world, which is a world of light and of sound. In his cry to return home to the one Source of all life he has tried to express the sound of the universe, which Plato called "the music of the spheres," in music, art, sacred architecture and geometry. Deep inside the soul there exists the knowledge that in order to build a better world, what lies within the heart of the universe needs to express itself here in the relative world. This can act as a signpost, pointing the way for all God's creatures who long to return through the Mother into a world of pure light whose expression is the sound that lies within the soul of souls.

In order to come to "hear" and to "see," the inner ear and the inner eye need to be opened. Paradoxically, "we" cannot open that ear and that eye. They are opened through an act of Grace. This is entirely dependent upon the amount of work we do upon ourselves as an obligation to fulfill the destiny of life on Earth. Work on ourselves means working with our *nafs* or lower nature, sometimes called the carnal soul, which initially does not want to see, does not want to hear.

Our life here on Earth is maintained through the transformation of subtle energies. It is a form of alchemy—a process through which and within which there may eventually come a fusion of the higher and lower worlds. It is at that point of fusion that the inner eye and the inner ear are opened. Sometimes on the way we are granted glimpses into the other world. These are "tastes" given to us through Grace, showing us that we are indeed traveling the way of love, compassion, and service. The straight way leads us to everlasting life, not everlasting life "after" this moment, but within this eternal moment, which is the only moment there is.

In the Sufi tradition we often talk about the "rain." We say that there is another world which has another sun and another sky. The rain that falls from that world is the rain of Grace that brings about the transformation of man. If we look to our everyday world alone, we will not be open to receive that Grace. Equally, if we do not yet realize that that rain from the other world needs also to fall here, so that the new age, called the second cycle of mankind, may come into being, then we only fulfill one-half of the opus or great work that the alchemists have talked about. The "rain" falls from the light, containing within it the first sound. It manifests itself in music and the expression of music in the form of pure geometry. Initially it might be hard to relate music to geometry. In the same way that every note has a particular vibration and waveband extending from a point which is the first note, so all geometry starts from one point and extends to another point creating a light, until the brilliance of the geometry of the perfect crystal is made manifest.

We are talking about sound and the possibility of being so attuned that we can be open to this rain from the other world. It is said, "Take one step towards God and He takes ten towards you." Although He gives us everything, we have to make the first step on the path of return. We have to strike the first note. It is dependent upon the quality of the note we strike as to what is given to us in return.

For thousands of years, people have talked about the angels and the archangels. We have been told how the angels, within the science of angelology, are "helpers" towards the realization of unity. This science, although much forgotten, contains knowledge of music, since the angels are, in reality, harmonics in the musical note.

Obviously this will be difficult to comprehend if we try to understand the meaning of angels from a sentimental or childlike approach. If we could only listen, we would become able to hear the harmonics and the overtones returning at once from every note we strike, whether on a musical instrument or within the human voice, or even in our thoughts and feelings and gestures. God has no mouth but ours; He has no voice but ours. If we take that first step towards God in our passionate yearning to know the truth, so indeed it is His voice that reverberates in the notes we sing. Immediately, the angels, the "helpers," the harmonics of the first note struck, come into play.

The problem (a problem being merely an unattended situation) is that we are so identified with who and what we think we are, that we do not open ourselves to listen to the reply. Most of our lives we do not want to hear the truth. Instead, we want to have agreement given to our lower natures. We have endless arguments between each other's lower natures and that only brings forth confusion. Yet again, here is another paradox. Despite ourselves, whether we are awake or asleep, the harmonics come into play on every note that is struck. The harmonics, the angels, have only one desire in life (in the same way that thought forms have only one desire in life). They desire to manifest themselves through man, as a way to return to the one Source of all life. Can we imagine the confusion of sound if the harmonics clash together when trying to return through a group that wants only to argue and perpetuate the illusion of their own separate existence from God?

If we surrender who and what we think we are, we may come to such a perfect pitch of attunement that each note struck within us is an everlasting example of the first note, the first sound, from which all music extends. Hazrat Inayat Khan once said, "Let Thy wish become my desire." J. S. Bach once said, "When the right notes are struck at the right time, the instrument plays itself." We are the instruments of God. We must never forget this if we are to truly be of service. We could say also: "God hath no image but that He finds in man." (Rafi Zabor).

The question is—How exactly can we attune ourselves? Obviously, if we have a musical instrument, no good will come out of the instrument if it is not correctly tuned. We have the strings and the frame, and within lies the knowledge of the tuning of the instrument. Once the tuning is correct, not only can we experience the laws that govern our existence on Earth, but most certainly we will attempt to remain "in tune."

Now what is attunement? Various methods can be used. We can use sound—verbalized or silent. We can use breath. We can use meditation—whatever that means, as it has such a loaded connotation these days. Mainly we use breath and silence, inner silence and attunement, so that we can really hear the answer. Unless we can hear inwardly, we will not receive the answer. A lot of the work I am doing, particularly with young people, is in trying to help them get into their bodies. They sort of nest in the head. If you were to poke them in the leg, they would say "ouch" as a physical reaction, but they would not be aware of where they had been touched. The average person is simply not in his body. We need to learn to bring attention and energy to areas of the body in order to truly inhabit it.

Since the answer is here, we can only receive it to the extent that we are here. Commonly, the mind is thinking, "The answer may come." Just about the time we are getting bored, the answer *may* come. The mind is usually playing little games, going hither and thither. We need to inhabit our bodies, because the only ears God has are ours, and the only mouth He has is ours. God made man in His image. We know how difficult it is for us to be here, to be awake, in the present moment. Young people, particularly, are usually not firmly grounded in their bodies. I know they are not going to get the answer if they are not here. They will get what they think they need of it. The mind will take a little bit and say, "That's it, thank you very much for today." But they will never be able to apply action. They cannot use the answer, because action has to come through the physical form. It is not a mind thing. This is something for all of us to watch, because we are never going to get the real answer unless we are awake to our own present moment.

In any great art it is necessary that we become apprentices to that art form. In this world it takes time and practice to "make perfect." Even if we are given tastes along the way, it may take a lifetime of attempting to strike a note in perfect pitch before all the angels can sing in glorification. When the angels glorify God, they are glorifying God in man. The universe is made for man and there is no God but God!

The first step in attuning the instrument that we call "man" is to put ourselves in such a receptive space that we can then be "ready" to strike that first note. To see and understand the miracle of life, we have to be receptive to change. Here again, the key is to be receptive, to open ourselves, to allow ourselves to be "seen" and not to be frightened to be exposed to the truth. We are asked to be open, to be aware, to be in love with the Beloved with a passion that defies all reason. Reason is powerless in the expression of love. The expression of love that shatters the discursive mind is the music of life, the rain that falls from the other world, here and now, if we will only listen, if we will only be receptive and awake.

HUMILITY AND THE ACTION OF LOVE
"In order to love we have to consider two things: humility and time."

The first step towards complete love is true service, wherever we are and in whatever moment. This is to understand and assist the manifestation of God's beauty. Even if we do not yet know it, we can trust that there is only one absolute Being who may be served. He has already given us the laws to live by.

Mevlana said, "He creates good and evil, but receives only good." Evil brings us into the unpleasant condition of separation, so that through that pain we may finally be motivated to return. Sufism is called the path of return. In this way we begin to love, so that eventually we can say, "Wheresoever you turn, there is the face of God." Once we enter this path, even if we put only one toe in this river while nobody is watching, we come under laws different from those under which the average human being lives. To come to love completely we have to obey those new laws, which are not forms, but the inner pattern for God's work. There are simple laws like beginning meetings on time and doing what we say we will do in the right time. Who really is speaking in us when we promise something? Who says I will? We will find that every time we do not do what we say we will, things go wrong. From potential love and light, we wind up in chaos. It is hard to love in that condition. There are basic laws that we need to understand and live by in order to love completely. One aspect of love is order, or law-conformability.

We pray, "Direct us in the straight path, the path of those to whom Thou hast been gracious, not the way of those from whom Thou hast turned Thy Face, nor of those who go astray." The only reason to be on the path is to love completely, because this is a path of love. Who and what brought us here in the first place? God Himself says, "I was a hidden treasure and I longed to be known, so I created the world that I might be known."

In order to love completely we need to consider two

things—humility and time. Humility makes us receptive and soft to the action of love. Then, we wait until the time is right. However, waiting is not in time, but in the eternal present, without expectation. "Expectation is the red death." An immediate decision is required; the decision to be humble and to see the action of love in that moment. If we want to help someone, we do not create a state of expectation in the person. When we are in expectation, we are liable to pick up a cold or something similar. It is like riding on the front of a sailboat instead of handling the rudder. In the early stages, expectation is useful. In fact, most spiritual schools attract people with all sorts of expectations. We hope to come to knowledge of objective hope which goes beyond expectation to see what is really hopeful in a situation.

One trap is looking for results, saying, "If I do this, the result will be good; and if I do not do this, the result will be bad." These are expectations, "the red death." Even healing can be another trap. Suppose a course of treatment is given and something happens. Another treatment is then given and soon a state of perpetual expectation develops. It just goes on and on; the present moment is never faced.

To love completely we have to be in the present moment, because there is only this one moment. Bring the matter to decision immediately. Do not hesitate; take courage. Without this decision, expectation is perpetuated. There is no blame when there is no knowledge. The great teachers I have been privileged to meet, in the Middle East, England, and America, were extraordinary because they never produced this state of expectation. There was therefore no spiritual ambition. Spiritual ambition comes from lack of knowledge and there is a lot of it around.

Another aspect of love is loyalty, in the mystical sense of the word. One can be loyal to knowledge and truth. Knowledge and truth inevitably lead to love. If we break the shell and find the kernel, we receive spiritual communication. Knowledge is given and not acquired. We can "work on ourselves" to break the shell, so that the knowledge can be given that leads to love. We may find the kernel and hear its tale. What is needed to break the shell is the formation of right motives outside of habitual responses. With right motive and intention, the very act of decision breaks the shell of conditioning and allows the raw kernel to be in that moment. It is not a sequential process. Loyalty has to do with law, decision and intention. It is an act of will, beyond ourselves, and it breaks our shell. This process awakens our inner perception. We begin to hear the voice of the kernel and to taste the kernel itself. "Were it not for the sweetness of the kernels, who would listen to the rattling voices of the walnut shells?"

The shell is a form which has endured so that we may silently come to know the kernel. If we are trying to do something, it just rattles the shell. If we wish to come to love, we must relax into a deeper level of ourselves, within all the shells, beyond the shells. By allowing the shell to be cracked in a way that we are not cracked along with it, we may relax and soften or melt, and the shell can be removed more easily. Allow, allow it.

When we know love, that is the day of recognition. This used to be called the day of reckoning or judgment, the day of blood and thunder. Now it is called the day of recognition, of "re-knowing." If we did not already know, we would not be traveling toward that point. The essential substance of the soul is knowledge. The soul knows where it is bound. But we have to find our soul, because the soul is made up of the knowledge that inevitably leads to love. To find the soul we must allow the shell to be broken.

TYPES OF FOOD *"Only through human beings can food of all types be redeemed, transmuted, and brought into Spirit."*

I want us to understand that we are a composite manifestation of a moment in time. That is all that we are. If we are not awake to this moment, then we are splattered across the universe in a state of chaos. We are not then fulfilling our function in being born man and woman. If we are awake, if we are free, we will finally manifest the need of the moment, because it can be nothing else but that.

Most people do not want to be awake. They think they want to be awake, but they do not actually want this. They think a teacher is going to give them something, but everything that is needed has already been given and only needs to unfold.

A teacher can, in a sense, provide us with a certain type of food. There is the physical food that we eat and there is also the food of impressions coming through awareness. In eating a carrot, much more is coming through the carrot if we are awake to the color of the carrot and to many other things. Also, there is food through the word. Within the word and within each moment, all truth is contained. He has limitless attributes and each attribute is shown through His Name; each word is His Name. Each word, each name, each phrase can be vital for understanding. People think they have an intuition of the truth, but we know nothing in this world unless we are told it. We can experience it within, but until somebody comes to confirm it in this world, we do not know it. That is why to miss a chance to be together is a tremendous waste.

The average human being stuffs food down one end and excretes it out the other. That is all he does and it keeps him going. The possibility exists that he may have an impression. He might eat in silence and feel the impression of that coming through. If he is in a state of love, he may also realize that he is redeeming that which he eats. So, to the extent to which he is awake to impressions, to his breathing and other things, he takes in a further form of food.

The other type of food can only come when we are awake to the words spoken from and through an individual who has reached a point of freedom, who is manifesting that which is necessary and true. Then there is a possibility of a whole human being, a wholeness coming into play. If we understand life and really come into yearning, what is it we want? We want the word of truth. We want confirmation of the truth within us.

We need to learn how to eat properly. We also need to purify the *nafs*, the false ego. This is not done by fighting it with negative things but by working with the positive. Little by little we become clear channels for what is called in the Sufi tradition the "light of pure intelligence." It comes when we eat the food in a state of love. Only then can we share what comes through the word. Otherwise it is prattle and means nothing at all. What is contained in the word is potentially the most important thing in this world. It will manifest in each of us differently, in the unique aspect of God as one within the One.

The food we take in is so important. It cannot be stressed enough. When we feed the body, we need to be awake to the knowledge that through love, by loving and because of love we redeem that which we eat. There are two sorts of screams a carrot can make. One is, "It hurts;" the other is, "Thank God." There are two sorts of screams you make if I attempt to heal you. One is, "Let me out of this;" the other is, "Thank God, here I go." There are two sorts of screams we can make each moment of our lives. One leads us to redemption and finally to resurrection. A seed can be sown where there is land it can grow in. The other is a scream of pain and all the things that go with it because we will not let go, we will not surrender and we will not be awake to the need.

Impressions are living beings without the degree of consciousness needed to know what is necessary. Only through human beings can food of all types be redeemed, transmuted, and brought into Spirit. Otherwise it is the endless process of the continuous, unpleasant scream. What we eat through the word is the food needed for the seed within us to grow. Otherwise it will not grow. It cannot grow without that which comes through the word.

THE RECOGNITION OF TRUTH *"For our inner being to know the truth, a mirror is required."*

Study is not intellectual, though without the intellect it is impossible. It is motivated by love, the love of the one Truth to know Itself. We could say it is only the truth that loves to know the truth. It is because of beauty that the truth recognizes itself. This is the beauty of the perfection which is discovered when that which is sought and that which seeks are recognized to be the same.

To take a very simple example, when we recognize a form to be beautiful, for instance, a flower, it is the inner essence of our being, our truth, that recognizes the inner essence of the flower, its truth, as essentially the same truth. The recognition takes place through the medium of the form of the flower. We could say: truth has recognized itself; its measuring rod was beauty and its mirror, the form of the flower.

This points to a simple fact. For our inner being to know the truth, a mirror is required; or, put in another way, the essence discovers itself in the mirror of form. The converse of this is also true, which is a paradox to ponder over and which provides yet another entry point or insight. For us, as a separate form, to recognize any other separate form, such as a flower, requires the truth, which is beyond form. The truth serves as a mirror in which it is seen; otherwise, it would have no existence. This mirror may not be known to be there, but without it no forms could appear.

Thus, when we study the truth beyond the confines of form, we require a mirror in which it may be reflected and through which it may be recognized. Conversely, when we study this form, which reflects the truth, we discover that it exists because of the truth, which is beyond form.

When a pupil is guided on a path of spiritual development, that which guides becomes for the pupil the mirror through which the pupil recognizes his own essential self. That which guides comes to be recognized as the form which reflects the essential truth and is determined by it.

Such a guide may be a person, or it may be a life situation, or it may be the written word. It is certainly true that, when we study the writings of a mystic who has realized the essential truth and whose writings come from that Source, then our guide can be either the mystic or that by which he was guided. He combines an essential reflection of the truth, with the situation in which we find ourselves while studying, and the written words we are studying. All these together will act as a mirror in which Truth recognizes Itself. When it is love that dedicates our study, that is when it is wholehearted.

God says, "I was a hidden treasure and I longed to be known, so I created the world that I might be known." If the form of the world is such that God ceases to know Himself in it, then that form ceases to exist. It is becoming increasingly obvious that the only form of the world that is not doomed to cease is one which allows man a universal understanding based on true knowledge born of love.

The Divine Essence, conceived of apart from the immanent aspect, is unknowable except to the Essence itself. It is in that sense that God says, "I was a hidden treasure and I longed to be known, so I created the world that I might be known." (*hadith* of the Prophet Mohammed, may the blessings and peace of God be upon him). To ordinary man, each form in the universe, including himself, hides the Divine Essence. He can worship God as a transcendent Being who stands outside himself and the forms of the world, but he may not know Him as the unity of the immanent and the transcendent aspects within himself and everything else. Each form in the universe is capable of revealing the Divine Essence that gives it existence, and each part of the whole is capable of revealing the whole. It is only a gnostic, however, who can see and know what is revealed. From this point of view, God can be considered to be a rational principle and an all-knowing essence. Man, as a part of the whole, has, as his essence, the same rational principle that gives him existence and through which he can know himself. Thus, when man comes to know himself, Unity knows Itself, and God can say to the man who knows himself, the perfect man, "It is because of thee that I created the universes." It is in this sense that the perfect man is known as the guardian of the world.

Thus, man can be seen as the link between the immanent and the transcendent aspects of God. He stands between Heaven and Earth and can know both, but this demands that he loves God in all His aspects, immanent and transcendent, both outside himself and within himself. Put differently, the Unity loves and knows Itself beyond all aspects through the perfect man who embodies that unity.

THE SOLE PURPOSE OF LOVE IS BEAUTY
"The observer and the observed become one."

There is always a very great danger of our getting into comparison. It is the same if we compare yesterday with today, or yesterday with what we expect to come out of tomorrow, or indeed almost anything. "Beauty is in the eye of the beholder." What is beautiful to one person might well not be beautiful to another. It is possible to see that the "beholder" is in actuality the Beholder. That is, we become the agents of His Grace, bringing forth the latent beauty that lies everywhere by giving agreement to it. After all, a mineral does not know that it is beautiful, nor does a beautiful tree or a rose bush, nor does a lion understand the beauty of a man or a woman. It is only man who can bring forth this latent beauty in all things, and how little he does it! He may go to a zoo and see the majesty of the animals and the birds. He may look at picture books. He may look out of his window into the garden and wonder at the beauty of a spring day. Yet all of this is useless if he does not bring out the beauty that lies dormant within each human being. Therein lie all the kingdoms, the mineral and the vegetable and the animal, all waiting to be set free into a beautiful world through our recognition.

When we are in a state of comparison, we cannot see the essential beauty. How can we say that a Van Gogh painting is more beautiful than a Breughel, or a piece by Mozart is more beautiful than one by Ravel? We can say that we prefer this piece to that piece, for whatever reason. That is an intelligent thing to do. We can make a choice as to what we wish to do, which road we wish to follow, and with whom we choose to journey. But if we go into comparison, we might spend the rest of our lives without knowing where we are going, what we want to do, or what is beautiful for us.

The following are three tools we can use to help us resolve the confusion in which we may find ourselves. First, we are foolish if we compare one cycle, one octave, with another. The octave starting with middle C, for example, may sound similar to another one starting with a higher C note. They are not the same. Each serves different purposes. How can we compare a minor with a major scale? It just does not work. Secondly, please remember that the pyramid is built from the top down. Only those who are far above us can view the whole of the mountainside from the vantage point of the peak, and thus see people both climbing up and climbing down. Those going up and those returning are seen to be equally important. Thirdly, although we are asked to remember that everything takes time in the relative world, the amount of time will depend on both the amount of effort we put into each thing we do and the degree of our patience and perseverance. Patience is not a passive state, but rather an actively receptive state.

How can we recognize the beauty of life? We stretch our hand out to a rose and listen to what it says to us. We listen to the effect inside of ourselves without judging at all. We feel what it is like inside ourselves to have confronted the rose. We bring into play all the senses we can and become highly sensitive to the rose. Such attention may release a type of energy that is beyond the stage when there is just the rose and he who observes the rose.

The moment we reverse the flow of energy and listen to what the rose says to us, we bring the surroundings into perspective. Try it. By reversing the flow so that we listen inside to what the rose is saying to us, our vision seems to expand. We become aware of the space in which we and the rose are together. We start to listen, see, feel, taste and touch the God in the rose and in us. Although there is still duality at this stage, and there surely is, we are bringing greater per-spectives of vision into play.

The next stage of awareness occurs when we are aware of the flow of energy between the rose and ourselves. Now we bring in the third part, the observer. There is something in us which is always able to observe. Here we do not identify with the rose at all. We see it in all its beauty. We do not judge it from conditioned mind, saying it is this, or it is that. We just see it as it is and observe ourselves being aware of it. Instead of just the room coming into focus, suddenly something else does too.

What a beautiful rose it is; what new things have suddenly unfolded in our lives. Have we ever at that point been more aware of the nature of the petals? How each one folds into itself? Have we ever been more aware of the fact that this vehicle that sees the God in the rose is the same vehicle through which the rose is able to feel God? Now the rose literally becomes more beautiful because we give the rose the loving attention it deserves without judging it and thus humil-iating it.

The fourth stage of awareness occurs when we are aware of the fact that we are observing the rose, what it says, and the flow of energy between it and us. We are now aware of the whole history of the rose. By observing one petal, we are observing the whole nature of the rose from its source to its bud, to its growth, creation and opening into flower. Our awareness level is heightened to a tremendous degree.

The fifth stage occurs when the observer and the observed become one. There is complete knowledge that I am rose, I am flower, I am mineral, I am animal, I am buried in the wind, I am the wind in the sky, the stars, the moon. All form is my seeing of God, and all sound is my hearing of God. In fact, God sees through me, hears through me, touches through me. Let Thy word become my speech, Beloved, and Thy love become my creed.

When we have reached beyond the nature of even knowing God as within, without identification, there is the sixth plane of consciousness. That sixth plane is where creation takes place. Creation takes place beyond the relative world. Perhaps now we understand why so much stress is being laid on the nature of awareness. When we walk along the street we may realize now that we are only sleepwalking. What about when we make love? What about when we apparently are in a great state of exaltation? Are we really aware or are we identified?

When a dervish greets another dervish he does not say, "How are you?" The dervish bows and then he says, "How wonderful to see God made manifest in your eyes." Then the second dervish might reply, "Ah, if it were not for the love in your heart it would not be possible for you to see God in my eyes." "Ah," the first dervish might say again, "But if it were not for the divine love shown through you, it would not be possible for you to say how it was that the love was showing in my heart." "Ah," the second dervish might say, "If it were not for the divine presence we could not be aware of each other." They would then embrace and go their ways. The divine presence is everywhere always at the same time. It has always been; it will always be. Nothing is lost in the Absolute; it is always there. When we are aware, we are in love.

First, we come to be in love with life through the rose, the tree or the plant. Then, perhaps, we come to be in love with God through human beings. And then, perhaps, we come to be in love with God by being in awareness of life itself. We shout to the heavens, "I am in love, I am in love. Oh, I am so in love because I am aware of God in every single moment of my life, in every second of my living life I see Him. I see Him in the trees. I see Him in the plants. I see Him in everything. I feel Him in everything. I touch Him in everything. I taste Him in everything. I hear Him in everything. How can I not be in love?"

When there is suffering, I do not say it is me that is suffering. I say, "No, it is God that suffers, that His rose bush may be pruned, that a rose may grow, a beautiful rose." To be aware we must work. There is no easy path. One flash of awareness may change man's attitude but it does not teach him to be aware all of the time. That is work. One flash of love does not teach him the nature of desire that traps him from being awake to the needs of the present moment. We must work and listen within to what life is telling us. Instead of projecting outwards, we listen inwards. We must learn to wake up every moment of our lives.

Have we ever thought what it would be like to listen inside to what was being said by somebody apparently outside? Think about it. When we attend a concert of music by Bach, there is no point in just staring at the orchestra pit and listening outside. Listen to the beauty of Bach within. What about listening within, all of the time, to what the world is telling us, whether it is in the words of man, or the crying of the wind in the trees, or a baby's smile? Listen within to what is said, and the truth will be revealed. We reverse the senses because we find the truth within.

There are two sorts of space. One, I call centric space. It can be seen in symbolic form as a circle, with a dot in the middle and lines radiating out from the center to the periphery. The center is saying "I" and the response is "me." Ninety-nine percent of human beings live in this space and believe that they can, in one sense, be the cause of something. The unawake man says, "I am doing this. I am not doing this. I think this is good. I do not think this is good. I am seeing that. I am listening to you, Reshad." This is judging from centric space, which is our viewpoint most of our lives.

There is another viewpoint called peripheral space, represented by a spiral leading towards the center. If we could get into that space now, quite quickly, we could learn more. The way to hear is to reverse space. That is when we know our dependence upon God and our total uselessness in terms of being the cause of anything.

We are the composite manifestation of a moment of time. We are becoming from Being. The only way to unlock the universal memory is to realize we are heard. In peripheral space, we no more say, "I see, I hear, I listen, I touch, I smell." We say, "I am heard, I am touched, etc." We are completely humble in that state. When we know we are heard, we can hear. When I say, "Do not speak unless you are spoken through," what I am really saying is to be in peripheral space. What comes through this vehicle to share is in response to the questions, spoken or unspoken, which are being asked. This space is not, "I am looking at a tree," but "I am seen by the tree." Not "I am listening to you," but "I am heard." There is a great Sufi saying: "There is no creation in the relative world, there is only the becoming of Being."

In peripheral space, everything starts to change. If we were to go into the woods, for instance, walking gently and beautifully, the different greens would permeate us through the degree of our love. It is an altogether different way of living. The purpose of it is to realize that in reality there is only unity. We must come back to unity. We must remind ourselves that although all the techniques for healing can be useful, unless we remember God and remember unity, we can get lost a short way up the mountain.

The object of the proceedings is the union of these two viewpoints. This is the great key. It looks like a spider's web. It is the spiral leading to the center and the radial lines leading out. In that space we can really say there is only Him; there is only God. It is becoming from being. The split second between the bud and the rose is known only by those who have become roses.

CONSCIOUS SUFFERING *"Conscious suffering is inevitable if we give our lives to a life of service."*

On the way there is pain. There is pain because we have said "I will." But the pain itself is really an illusion, because God never wanted us to suffer. There is no need for this at all. What He is, and what the experience is of the magnificence and the glory of God, is nothing but joy. Our obstinacy and arrogance bring about pain that we do not want for each other and that He does not want for us. Joy is like a mother. It hurts to have a baby, but the extraordinary joy of birth comes through this. We are basically being asked to give birth to our real self. Each one of us comes upon who and what we are in that act of surrender.

If we truly know who we are, a whole galactic system bursts into life. It is not as though it is something new, because all creation is in one moment. We are merely fulfilling something that was set in motion at the beginning of time, in the first Word of God. Let us not misunderstand about pain; finding God does not have to be heavy. It does not have to involve walking around in a state of "Am I doing the right thing?" It is a question of building the yearning. The distance between us builds the yearning to touch. On whatever level, the distance between each one of us and that one Source of all life, builds the yearning to die and be assimilated into what we call the Divine Presence. The pain we feel can turn into joy very easily. The pain we feel, each one of us, is the pain of separation. We never have been separated and we never will be. We have always been one with Him. All we need is the knowledge of that. The first thing we need is knowledge— knowledge of ourselves. For this we have to do certain work. And along the line we come upon the idea of conscious suffering.

Conscious suffering is one of the greatest joys in the world; it is not painful. We are the instrument, the vehicles through which He sees and hears. We are the vehicles through which it is possible for transformation to take place. And that sort of suffering is another matter altogether.

The basic thing I am trying to point out is that if we turn straight to the one cause of all life, as a rose turns towards the sun, then we see the pruning and the bleeding and the suffering as an integral part of it all. These states of suffering are only temporary, but the mind cannot cope with that idea. It really cannot accept the fact that this temporary suffering need not last.

In our work together there will be states of great tension, but not a negative tension. These states just arise, coming upon one person one day and one person another, or the whole group for a period. If we can get that firmly fixed in our minds then we can go on. We can continue the work towards the aim that one day each one of us will be capable of holding 1000 people. And if one of us cannot, then four or five together can.

We may see the value of this when we begin to realize the implications of what we are doing and that there are so few of us.

Let us consider very carefully the meaning of pain and conscious suffering as we go about our daily work. If you see somebody in a state of pain or confusion, hold that person's hand. We need each other, right? He needs us, we need each other. Do not ignore the person. Equally well, do not become identified. Sometimes just an arm around a shoulder or holding a hand in the love of God is all that is necessary. Allow that moment to be released. Allow something to go through. Let us not insulate ourselves or try to separate ourselves from each other. If we do, we are separating ourselves from Him, because there is only Him. Let us not for one moment encourage separation or come to a place where we cannot face the situation. If we see someone who cannot face it, then let us go to them and give them love and agreement and understanding. At that particular moment they are not able to let go.

Every time we judge we are in separation. Every single moment we put ourselves in judgment, on whatever level it is, we are in separation. And we pay the consequences every single time.

The next step is the hardest of them all. Can we forgive? Go back now to the beginning, to your family and friends, to the endless things, all the pain. If you were not in pain, you would not be here. That is your visiting card to truth. Can we turn to all that muck, all the pain, all the suffering, which we saw as negative until now? There is no need to say, "I forgive," just know that there is forgiveness for the world, all the bombs, all the crap you were put through in your life, the pain we all know. Forgive. Jesus told us, "Father, forgive them, they know not what they do." Could we have the humility to be like Jesus for just one moment? It is like being children, but also intelligent children. "Father, forgive them, for they know not what they do." Think of the rape of the Earth, the destruction of whole tracts of land, the pollution of oceans, rivers and air. Forgive all these who behave so badly, because until we learn to forgive them, there cannot be a new world.

This I know, and I say it quite consciously. Until we forgive, there will be no new world. Forgive ourselves. Forgive all the stupidities we make every day of our lives. Stop judging. Stop standing in the seat of judgment thinking we are anything.

Let us learn to forgive and love. Can we actually love? Love yourself, but not separate from Him. Then we can face each other, not as animals but as human beings. The result of our work is dependent upon the degree of realization and surrender. As we surrender we have realization. There is realization in surrender.

We are not the Judge. "The fear of the Lord is the beginning of wisdom." When we know we know nothing, there is the possibility that we can know something. There is no point in acquiring more and more information. It might merely cause more pain and confusion. Instead, let us allow ourselves to be brought to the point of perplexity or bewilderment. Then there is that split second between the bud and the rose, and something can come about.

Healing is making love, which is absolutely possible, possible on this Earth. Healing, whichever of His wonderful kingdoms, is bringing wholeness into fullness in a human being.

Pain and heaviness come from our refusal to literally be here now. That is all it is, just refusal to be here now. Who wants to be here now? Maybe I think I want to be here now because I want to get something out of it. If we are all totally here now we do not have to get anything out of it at all. We merely lose the illusion of even the very statement itself. If we are here now, there is no pain. There is only joy. There is only the longing to let it go on, to let it unfold. In our daily lives we can help others towards this realization, but the understanding of conscious suffering is beyond consciousness. No mind can interpret it. No opinion can create forms out of it. It is beyond these things.

Possibly one of the most beautiful acts in the world is conscious suffering, for it is the contribution we can make towards the reciprocal maintenance of the planet and the future of mankind. It is really the only thing that makes any sense. It is the contribution from knowledge, for knowledge.

That is the knowledge of Him, which is what was really asked of us from the beginning. This involves discernment.

There is a saying, "Stand in this world, but bow in the next." These words can help us to learn how not to judge in this world, and how true discernment can come about by accepting what is intended for us from higher worlds. Sometimes it is said that a true dervish is not responsible for his actions, for a true dervish is not separate from either the higher worlds or this world. He does not judge in this world but he has discernment. Even though his actions may seem illogical, they are not coming from a world based only upon the comparison that arises from our judgment in this world of what we consider to be right or wrong.

We may be afraid to take responsibility as we begin to understand that we are powerless in the face of God. How are we capable of making a decision to take a responsible action? Let us consider the word responsibility, the root of the word being "response." Now there are two things we can respond to; we can respond to need or we can respond to desire. Desire is the relative aspect of love. God is love. If we do not desire, how on Earth is He going to manifest anything through us? But this is one of the great paradoxes. We teach people to get rid of their own personal desires, which is correct. At the same time we say that if we do not desire, nothing is possible. We would just go round in circles. We want our desire to reflect His wish, so that there is no separation.

Taking responsibility for an action means taking responsibility for ourselves. There is a saying, "He who knows himself, knows his Lord." There is another saying, "Words spoken, action done." I must be responsible for every word I speak and every action I make. There is nothing outside this room. The whole world is here, visible and invisible, so I must be responsible. Yet our elemental nature does not want to be responsible, especially if it believes this to be painful.

People often ask if we have to recognize the pain before we can offer it up. This is not necessary. If we believe in Christ, this question does not arise. Christ is known as the redeemer of the world. We do not have to recognize our own pain, but we can allow it to be recognized. All the therapies in psychology of putting attention on our pains are merely lack of faith. If we allow ourselves to be recognized, we are allowing God to love us. In fact, we are loved. It might help to sit down and start to recognize things. But if we still hang on to the pain it does not help at all. What is asked of us is to allow ourselves to be loved, to allow ourselves to be redeemed. It is not a question of illusion being killed, because there is only Him. It is a question of the false being assimilated in the real.

When I work in healing, people come and say, "This is what is wrong with me," and I say, "Oh, rubbish! This is what you think is wrong with you." They say, "Oh, I know it is a psychological thing inherited from my parents." I say, "No, that is merely a symptom of a deeper pattern."

The recognition happens behind the form, beyond words. When there is recognition, there can come about redemption, if we will allow it to be so. Some of us may be able to see the cause behind the cause, but this perception cannot be forced. It is not necessary to recognize the pain because that is putting ourselves in judgment. Our lives in this world are a continuous state of suffering, mainly unconscious, until those times when we begin to be granted the knowledge of the purpose of life on Earth. Then suffering, which as I said is mainly unconscious, may become conscious.

When people come to see me, they come because of pain and because of suffering. It is not so difficult to alleviate the apparency of suffering. It is much more difficult to get people to see the purpose of suffering and how, through conscious suffering, they can begin to fulfill their obligations.

If suffering comes from the pain of separation and if we can accept and face the reality of God, then there is a purpose in the illusion of separation. If we are asleep we cannot see a purpose in life and we cannot see any purpose in suffering.

Conscious suffering is inevitable if we give our lives to a life of service. The moment that we no longer work for ourselves but for the total evolution of the planet, which we could term "the Divine Plan" or "Divine Will," it is inevitable that certain events will occur that will produce what appears to be the relative opposite in this world. When we truly give our lives to a life of service, we must not deny what will inevitably arise from that one total commitment to God. The understanding of the nature of the different laws that govern our destiny upon Earth is really given to us only when we have given our life away and, at the same time, accepted the inevitable result.

For now, let us see whether we are prepared to take that great step into the unknown, whether we are yet ready so totally to give away our lives. Giving away our lives does not mean that we lose anything. Rather, it means that at last we are granted something and are asked to examine how we might give away our knowledge as our act of service in His Name.

For many of us, the very idea of conscious suffering will be totally new. What would it mean to suffer consciously? It would mean suffering for another—when there is only He, the one absolute Being. Can we learn to suffer for God? What is the key to unlock this possibility—not as a so-called negative approach to the work of life on Earth, but rather as a truly positive approach to His will?

The key is knowledge, for love without knowledge is not enough. The experience of the energy of love can lead us to many states, but without knowledge of the purpose of life on Earth, little good will come of it. We may come finally to a sense of disillusionment, realizing that we have to keep repeating similar patterns until at last we can fulfill our obligation of being born man and woman on this planet. That obligation begins with this strange word, "knowledge."

Knowledge is given and not acquired. It is given only when we have worked on ourselves to be completely open to receive a taste of what our lives are all about. As we work on ourselves, we begin to discover that working *for* ourselves and our own self-development or growth is not totally satisfying.

Let us go back once more to the analogy of the baby in the womb of the mother. After the child is born and the cord is cut, the parents, if they are real parents, want only freedom for the child, freedom which perhaps they themselves have not yet been granted. So they set out to work to produce what is often called "a better life" for their child. For that, much sacrifice is necessary on every level, from the physical to the spiritual. The parents work to provide the best possible education for the child, bringing forth that which is within. If we could only consider the degree of sacrifice that parents need to make, that their children can make a better world, we might come to understand something of what is meant by conscious suffering. Parents are working now, not just for themselves, but for a new being born into the world. That being can only come to realize that there is no separation from the one absolute Being through the sacrifice of the parents.

We are the parents of a new age. In every moment we live and on each breath that we take, the infinite possibility of the realization of truth is here. If we are awake, if we are conscious and in knowledge, we are ever respectful to the need of the moment.

Paradoxically, there is no "reward" in conscious suffering. From the planting today, the harvest will be reaped when the time is right. We may never see the result ourselves. That does not matter. If it matters to us, then our actions are merely a projection of our lower nature which demands always to see the results.

Martin Buber, author of *I and Thou,* once explained that when we have taken this great step, this commitment, it does not make life lighter, but, rather, heavier—heavier with meaning. Once the commitment has been made by any of us, we enter into a new world. Within that world there are different laws, laws that do not apply to the average person without commitment. It is necessary that we come to understand what these laws are and to live by them. If we do not, then conscious suffering can be dangerous.

B REATH *"We can be born consciously, we can make love consciously, and we can die consciously. All these three are dependent upon one thing—breath."*

We can help in the overall plan of God by learning to breathe consciously every moment of our lives. Once we learn to control the breath, then we may find the rhythm of the Mother, the Creative Feminine, from whom we came and through whom we return to the one Source of all life. When we have the knowledge of the love between the Mother and the Father of all creation, conscious suffering becomes an act of joy.

In consideration of all that has been said, the question remains: Can we totally commit ourselves to a life of service? Until that commitment is made, we can only talk about what may lie beyond. We have to make the first step, and then the other steps are given, to the extent that we are completely honest and have the courage to face each moment.

The relationship to breath is very important here. If we are truly honest with ourselves (and honesty is a prerequisite of anyone wishing to understand the nature of the way of love), we know that we come into life on the breath and we go out of what we call life on the breath.

Consider the birth of a child. During the period in the womb, the breath of the child is the breath of the mother. Only when the umbilical cord is cut is the child breathing on its own. I wonder if we can imagine the shock all this entails and perhaps the intention behind that individual breath given at the moment when the child is separated from its mother. Maybe then we could see in our own lives the separation from the womb and the breath of the Mother herself.

We have two types of breath that are existent in every moment; the natural breath of the Divine Mother and the breath that we, in our illusion of separation, attempt to impose on life. If we can find the Mother's breath, that natural rhythm that exists in every moment, then we have the possibility of returning to the womb of the Divine Mother, from which we can be reborn. This is called the second birth. With that knowledge, we are eternally present and eternally being reborn with each breath we take.

When a woman gives birth naturally, it is necessary that she learn how to breathe. If we are the parents of a new age, and thus through alchemical fusion the mother of a new age, then it is equally necessary we learn the science of breath. The birth of a child is certainly painful in the physical sense. If we are totally conscious in the breath, we do not identify with the pain, and the child that is born, even at the moment of the cutting of the umbilical cord, knows deep within its soul that indeed there is no separation.

This is our challenge and our responsibility—to give birth to the child that we call the new age, realizing, first of all, that through the knowledge of breath we give the child the chance that has not been granted before; and, secondly, that through a completely unselfish attitude and through our conscious suffering, we may bring this child to fulfillment. Then there can be no going back. The result of all this is something the mind cannot understand. As Mevlana Jelaluddin Rumi says:

"Reason is powerless in the expression of love.
Love alone is capable of revealing the truth of love
    and being a lover.
The way of our prophets is the way of truth.
If you want to live, die in love.
Die in love if you want to remain alive."

We can be born consciously, we can make love consciously, and we can die consciously—the three possibilities. All those three are dependent upon one thing—breath. An animal (and the animal within us) cannot breathe consciously. Its instinct changes the rate of its breath. Man and woman have the possibility of breathing consciously. We can literally awaken and work with breath every day of our lives. What is more, unless we do and until we do, we are not conscious. We can get so led astray by phenomena—physical, mental, emotional, psychic—that we cannot breathe. We need an observer so that the breath becomes conscious and not merely instinctive.

All the studies we can make, all the endless techniques, exercises, visions, plans, all these things will not come into being without breath. It simply is not possible. Think about a baby being born, when the child is born gently. It is already "breathing" in the womb of the mother, the heartbeat of the mother, the womb of the moment. We are in exactly that position. There is the heartbeat of the Divine Mother in this moment of time. And we are being breathed, though we have forgotten what that means.

Death is a tyrant. But we must always keep death in mind. Although we have much to endure, it is nothing compared with dying. We are born on the breath, and we apparently die on the breath. If we are asleep in breath, we will die asleep. But if we are awake, it is said that we are born into eternal life. What are we here for? To be responsible human beings. All else means nothing. We can die consciously in breath. As we breathe in, all and everything is contained in that moment; and as we breath out, all and everything is settled in the place in knowledge where it should be. Our life is only important relative to the degree of our responsibility in God and all that this means. Without breath we will not learn.

We can choose the quality of air we breathe. That quality is dependent entirely upon our degree of awareness. There has to be a rhythm of breath, because there is the rhythm of the universe. Each of us is a cosmic apparatus for the transformation of subtle energies. That is what we are, and that is what we have to learn to be, through working with breath.

Through conscious breath we take in from the energies that God offers us every moment of our lives. If we do not take breath consciously, it is not surprising that we do not have the energy to make a commitment. If God made man in His image, then man can be conscious to breathe in from the six directions and include all the different kingdoms. If we breathe in from all directions and accept what God has given us, then we have the energy to make the commitment. Otherwise it is often a quasi-commitment. It is not real. The commitment may not go through.

Commitment cannot be real without breath, which has to

be balanced both ways—in and out. Most of us never breathe out at all. We breath in (wow!) or we get caught in the world of attraction (inward sigh, oh!). Our breath stops, right? Breath stops totally. We must learn to balance this by breathing out as well. We have to know when we are meant to be breathing *in* and when we are meant to be breathing *out,* on many levels.

Often we say we are going to do something yet we never complete it. Life is what we have to complete, because God gave us the possibility of completion in life. How can we possibly help other human beings unless we lead them, to the best of our ability, towards completion?

It is attention to breathing that is important. Every day, always try to take a little bit of time to breathe consciously. Never presume that our breath is always going to be just given to us, because one day it might be taken away. If we are going to become healers, conscious breath is vital. In the inner work our heartbeat and our breath will change. Therefore, try to take a little bit of time every day to pay attention to the breath.

M AKING LOVE *"Our life is to do with making love, and that means making love possible on Earth."*

We can increase our sensitivity so that it is like the Aeolian harp, perfectly strung and put on a mountain top, that resounds in perfect harmony when played by the wind. It is a wonderful challenge to get our whole being resounding in attunement to and resonance with the Highest. We often confuse the word consciousness with sensitivity. Sensitivity is our own, but consciousness is one of the energies already complete in itself. We cannot expand consciousness, because it is not ours. Becoming conscious means becoming awake. The best definition I know of is that consciousness is the reaction of active intelligence to pattern. We awaken intelligence through will, by applying will at the right time and at the right place.

I would like to reiterate that consciousness is a form of energy. It is not sensitivity to a part of ourselves or someone else, but the awareness of being aware. When we discover the nature of who and what we are, we tap the energy of consciousness, which is beyond mind. Through this there is the potential for the inflow of creative energy, the source of power through which life is generated. Within that is sexual energy, much discussed, much worried about. If we knew about who and what we are, then we would realize that the power of sex is quite another matter from what we think it is. It is beyond both sensitivity and consciousness. The creative carries with it unitive energy, which is really the redemptive spirit of God. This energy brings us to transcendent energy which we might call "the Divine Will." There is that which is still beyond.

When we meet it can be said that we are sharing love. Together we are sharing time and space. Something is being born. Something is being born now, through agreement, through our love, through our longing to love more and to know more. Something is being born that is the shape of the world to come. Making love with this in mind is quite another matter from what we so often do.

A child born out of love is a being made out of a special something which we call substance, which is produced through work on ourselves. We say that "the soul of man and woman is a knowing substance." It actually knows. The line that I am now apparently drawing in the air is made of a substance, which is there as long as I breathe. When we can understand this, whether we are talking about our relationships with our partners or whether we are talking about our relationship with our community, we will really meet. We will be sharing love together, and something can happen. We may not see it for a long time, but that which is born of this moment is exactly like a child who looks to his parents as God. Try and listen to what I am saying, because it is well worth contemplating now. A child sees its parents completely as God, and needs to be nurtured very, very carefully and regularly. As it grows up it has to have different sorts of caring. That being that I am talking about will grow to the extent that he or she is looked after. If we agree to what is happening right now in this space and remember the love that we are sharing, we are nurturing the future.

Making love is the most sacred act on Earth. There is nothing more sacred. Nothing. When we make love, we are at that moment of time, of our own volition, fulfilling the Divine Presence. What does it mean to make love? It means allowing God to make Himself love in us. Then we have transfiguration. If we will accept that we are making love when together, then we will leave each other transfigured. We are making love possible. We are making it possible for God to make Himself love in us.

Let us take the word "beloved." We say, "Beloved Lord, Almighty God." "Beloved" means "be loved." We allow ourselves to be permeated, transformed and transfigured in Love.

We wonder what to do with the energy that suddenly we are granted. Many people have been granted immense energy and do not know how to deal with it. Yet being granted this energy is not the problem. We are asked at this time to give our lives up totally to a life of service. If we do, the problem does not arise. This does not mean to say that there is not vast energy which we do not always know what to do with. But it is possible just to carry on and do what we have to do. There is an old saying—"Look after the little things and the big things look after themselves." We can look after the little things of life. For example, we wash the steps of our house every day, because we are asked to walk across the threshold and leave our past behind. We may look after the mineral kingdom, the plant kingdom, and the animal kingdom. The big things will look after themselves. If we can do this, then the question will not arise.

In the sky there is a dragon. Within ourselves there is a dragon. Saint George killed the dragon. Do not kill it anymore. Love sufficiently that the dragon is your friend. There is no more need to kill the dragon. The dragon is our friend. The dragon is the elemental world that comes up from the earth in fourness: fire, earth, air, and water. Ether carries it through. Until this point of history, due to the state of the relationship between man and woman, it was necessary to kill the dragon. It was necessary. Now it is not necessary. Let us say the spear of St. George is his own backbone.

Now is the time for woman, as herself in God. We men are asked to understand this very, very deeply. If we do, sex is on a totally different level. It is not a question of people experimenting with the body. It is not a question of feeling free because we can feel free to see the body. It is not a question of any of these things at all. It is a question of an inner knowledge, an immense respect and understanding of woman. Respect and understanding of woman will make sex one of the three creative acts that can bring about real change, as opposed to the apparency of change. Only the understanding of this can make it all possible. Let us use the energy we have been given to make love. It is a gift of God. Mevlana Jelaluddin Rumi says, "Love even turns copper into gold." Copper is Venus—the love play of Venus. Love even turns copper into gold.

It is said in our tradition, "Court the Beloved as you would your lover." Never let the Beloved leave your sight, your touch, your taste, your breath—any part of the gift we have really been given. Never let this be. Court the Beloved. It is a great courtship. What is courtship for? Courtship is a period before marriage. The Lord is the Beloved. It is neither male nor female, nor anything like that. The courtship is giving oneself in some inner realization and understanding that the Beloved means "be loved." Only when we have fulfilled our courtship can we be loved. Every woman knows that. No woman does not know it. Very few men know it. Pay court to the Beloved, who is forever formless. What is the result when the Beloved manifests His love in us? We are formless, because in fusion there is nothing left but what the Beloved gives to us. It is on that level that I want you to understand things. It is on that level that we have to learn patience. It is on that level that we have to learn to pass on whatever little we know about these things.

One day the planet will go back into the body of the sun. One day the Mother Earth will be fused within (not into, but within) the Father. One day the experiment of life on Earth will be fulfilled. Although I talk about our children and our children's children, I do not mean to say that we will not know it now. If we make love, we will know it. If we are making love now, we will know it now. If we are making love we will become transfigured in the knowledge of the love of God. The dragon in the sky is a blue spark of the invisible world. If we recognize that world in love, it can become our friend. If we do not, it can become our enemy, in the relative sense. When we make love the dragon is manifesting itself. There is no more time to kill the dragon. There is only time to know that the dragon is our friend.

Our life is to do with making love, and that means making love possible on Earth. The whole structure of one's body changes when one is in love, "in Love." Every cell has some consciousness of this and will change. Everything changes when we are in love. The planet, this beloved Earth, changes when we are in love. It cannot do this by itself. *We* have to. We have the possibility of being in love. Let us be in love every day, whether we have lovers or not. Whether we have a lover is not the point. The point is that when we are in love, wherever we stand or sit, wherever we walk, that is sacred ground.

D ESIRE *"Love is the cohesive force in the relative world, manifested through desire."*

In the spiritual work it is necessary to consider the nature of love and desire more closely. In almost all schools one of the first teachings is the transmutation of desire. But what is desire? What do we mean by saying, "I desire something?" What is this "I" that could desire anything in the first place? Desire itself is not one thing, but is comprised of seven major stages in the relative world.

Desire can be related to the seven centers, or energy wheels. These psychic centers have their counterparts in the physical form of the human body, and in the subtle bodies of man, which could be called the subtle anatomy of the body of God. They have a positive and a negative aspect; each has a color, a number, and a note of the musical octave associated with it. Each of them is involved in some way with the nature of desire.

In the base of the spine center, or the center representing the lowest element of animal man, we see the first stage of desire. The purpose of this center is the creation of form. In order to create, there must be three forces present—active, passive, and allowing. The number is three. The desire for form manifests itself in the relative world as the desire for big houses, for wealth, or for material objects. It is through these desires that we subconsciously attempt to prove that we exist. The real "I" does not need any proof of its existence but itself. Desire from the lowest center can be seen in the demand for form, the heaviness of gravity, and the importance placed on the material world. Without this desire there would be no creation of forms, no continuity, and no manifestation on the physical plane. So we cannot say that it is wrong. We can, however, build for God instead of for ourselves.

The color of this form of desire is red and it is related to the planet Mars, the god of war. I desire to take money from some other country and thus make my country rich. What I am doing is trying to prove my existence through force.

The base of the spine center is the area of the body where we excrete or get rid of expended physical energy. Yet it is also there, in the trinity of the number three, that creation starts in the physical world. We can notice how everything has its so-called good and bad aspects, and how one thing is necessary for the other to exist. Some people never get beyond this first desire for form. An example of this is the rich business man who becomes stuck on this level of desire and is finally not even interested in making love. He thinks only of making money or of making bigger buildings or more ships, or whatever.

The next stage of desire is involved with the nature of sex, the reproductive energy. This is what we most typically see as desire. Much of Western civilization, if we think about it, is built around sexual desire. Most advertising uses this. Sexual desire is one of the main forces to which man is a slave. Equally well, if man did not desire to reproduce himself, there would be no children in the world. Again, the desire involves another way of trying to prove that we exist.

We must never lose sight of the fact that love manifests in the relative world through desire. But love destroys and sacrifices that which it approaches through desire. What is normally meant by "I love you" is that I wish to possess you so that I may not have to face myself. Very seldom are we advanced enough to realize that I am loving the God in you. Therefore, I must also love the God in me. This is the union between human beings that we are looking for in the relative world.

This desire relates to the number four. For two people to reproduce themselves in the relative world, there have to be two physical forms doubled, i.e., each physical form, which consists of both heaven and earth, must be doubled. Thus we have the marriage of two heavens and two earths to make one new being. The four makes the three come into existence, or we could say that four makes the force of the trinity come into existence.

Orange, the color of this second type of desire, is the color of the germ of creation. It is the energizer of the world and energizes all the other energy wheels. On its lowest level, orange is violent and burns us. On its highest level, the result is the light of fire. When we strike a match it burns orange, but in a darkened room it manifests as light. When the desire of the color orange is transmuted in the heart, it radiates out from the heart in the form of light. That is, of course, when it becomes transmuted into pure love.

The next stage of desire, which is seen through the solar plexus center, is the desire to be recognized through emotion or through the emotional body. Its color is yellow. Yellow is the color of both wisdom and fear, two opposites. When man understands the nature of the emotional body or the subtle body which is connected to emotion, he becomes a wise man. The number is five, the five-pointed star, which is the symbol of man with his feet on the earth, his arms raised towards heaven and the light coming down from above. In black magic this symbol is reversed. The black magician wishes to trap people through fear, which is the reverse of wisdom.

We are all familiar with this form of desire. We feel that dig in the solar plexus when we do not get what we want. We desire something emotionally. For example, I may desire to buy a bunch of flowers more than anything in the world. When I get to the shop and find it closed, I feel bitter disappointment in the solar plexus from not getting what I desire.

Consider it again in the nature of love. If it were not for this sort of desire we would not have much of the great creative work that is being done in the relative world. If it were not for the nature of man wishing to prove that he exists through his emotional being, we would not have some of the great composers or the great artists of our time.

The next stage of desire is related to the heart center and is the desire to attract magnetically, whether consciously or unconsciously. The number is six, and its color is green. If I am not as attractive as someone else, I become "green with envy." If, on the other hand, I understand the nature of the heart, I understand that green is the catalyst in the color spectrum. It is neither positive nor negative; it is precisely in the middle. Green symbolizes the birth of spring and birth of all kinds. We have been asked to transmute the red, orange, and even yellow of the lower centers into the heart. If we use and understand the heart center well enough, it will attract the lower energies to itself and transmute them.

The heart center is very important. It is possible for a person to accelerate the nature of this desire by mistake and thereby become very magnetic. An example of this is a person who attains a degree of spiritual realization and attracts many followers to himself and then becomes blocked by his desire or magnetism from progressing further on the path.

The fifth stage of desire, and the last that is easily recognizable, is related to the throat center and to the color blue. This level of desire is more difficult to understand than the others, but it is still discernible by relative man. It could be called the desire of the word or the desire of vibration. Blue can reverse itself into depression, yet its true meaning is the exhaler of the world. If the limited "I" wishes to possess through communication and does not get what it wants, and of course eventually it will not, the color reverses and the result is depression.

This particular area, whose number is seven, is called the gateway of the soul. It is a crucially important center. It is where the "I" first starts to manifest itself in the relative world. It is said in the Bible, "In the beginning was the Word, and the Word was with God." When we say "I will" we cannot help but bring the "I" into manifestation. We start losing sight of what happens beyond the "I."

We can say that these five stages of desire are related to God immanent on Earth. These stages are characteristic of man in the relative world, forgetting that from which he came. They are, once again, the desire for form, the desire to reproduce oneself, the desire to be recognized through emotion, the desire to attract magnetically, and the desire of the word. We can be in all the stages at once, or we may become trapped in one or more stages of desire. We can only look at ourselves and try to see where we are trapped.

The next stages are equally important to understand, but because we can only look at them from our limited point of view, we cannot really understand the true meaning behind these planes. The next center is often called the "third eye." The number of this center is eight, which is the number of change, as in the *I Ching,* and the number of eternity when it is written sideways. Time and eternity are synonymous, and both exist in the relative world. We must realize that God, the Absolute, manifests Himself in the relative world through time. Time exists only through the nature of desire, because time moves forward in a clockwise direction and so does desire. Eight begins a new octave of existence. This plane of consciousness, which we call the causal world, corresponds to when "God says, 'Be' and all becomes," as stated in the *Koran.* It is like the knights in the Arthurian legends who went down on one knee and swore allegiance, agreeing to take part in the fight for the cause of light over darkness.

This center, which is connected with the planes of light, also has its opposite. That is why it is called the "evil eye" when its power is misused. Does this mean "eye" or "I"? Perhaps it means both. It is from this center that man is trapped if its power is misused. It is also the center of pure perception, clairvoyance, and pure clarity of understanding. It is the center where the will of God is made known on Earth. But it can still be involved with desire in the relative world. Man desires to have power, and this is the center of power. If he did not desire to have power, wheels would not turn.

The next center is related to the crown chakra. It has the number nine, which is the number of the Holy Spirit. It is difficult to see how we can desire the Holy Spirit, but we can. As long as we desire to see God, we can never find Him. In its positive aspect, one could say that at this plane God shows us how He participates in the dance of the planets. We understand this by participating and sharing in this dance, thus discovering that in fact it is God participating through us. It is a very important stage of consciousness and represents the element of God Transcendent. Its color is violet, the last color that we can see with the naked eye.

Love is the cohesive force in the relative world, manifested through desire. It is love manifested as desire that makes the world go round. Love itself has only one great purpose, and that is beauty. Now perhaps we can see finally how desire must be assimilated into the One, which is love. God is Love. It is necessary for God to manifest Himself in the relative world and for us to offer up our desire on the altar of His love.

B REAKING THROUGH SEPARATION *"Only by being in harmony with the Divine Principle can we exist with order in a chaotic world of disorder."*

We are continuously becoming in the relative world. We are becoming from two aspects simultaneously—from the past conditioning of our lives and from the higher vibrations.

Heaven is being brought to Earth, as Earth is turning into Heaven.

The first basic premise is that all matter is the result of the crystallization of light. The second premise is that thought emerging in the mind of man has already been becoming through other planes, which man in his present unenlightened state is unable to experience. And the third premise is that even the emotions man experiences, although they appear to be related to the relative world, are still mostly the results of higher forms of experience.

We are part of the universe, and the universe is part of us. We do not realize that our emotions are like the tides of the sea, which are affected very deeply by other worlds. We neither look up, nor do we look down, to see from where we are becoming. Man has forgotten that he is part of the growth of planet Earth. He has forgotten the sanctity of life and the planet from which he is continuously becoming, just as he has forgotten the nature of Heaven. One of our jobs in this new age is to teach people the miracle of life through living experience.

There are a series of interpenetrating bodies, bodies of energy, which are not separated from each other. For Heaven to come on Earth and for Earth to turn into Heaven, higher man, seen as a triangle with its point facing downward into the heart, must descend to Earth. Earth, with the point of its triangle facing upwards, must ascend into Heaven. Thus the great six-pointed star, which is the Seal of Solomon, is formed.

The key to this could be what we call the "dome," which is formed of numerous subtle vibrations or "veils," existing between the solar plexus and the heart. It exists just above the lower man and is really there for man's protection. Why is there this protection? If all of the conditioning of the past were instantly stripped away, what would man have to hang on to?

The key to the breaking of these veils lies in the fact that the dome represents the virgin. The virgin, in this sense, must be penetrated that the child may be born. The child here, of course, is the child born in the heart of mankind: the second coming.

When the heart is open we may see that immanence and transcendence are one, the two worlds are one. Then it can be truly said, "I saw a new Heaven and a new Earth . . . the old Heaven and the old Earth are passed away." The pain of separation, expressed by the flute and the reed, slowly and then more rapidly disappears. "Be ye as a little child," Christ said. When the child is born, I believe it has virtually no dome, only a little protection. Slowly, as we grow older, we build the dome through our sense of separateness in the universe and the other great illusions. The child does not see the separation of Earth and Heaven. When the new child is born in the heart, man becomes the new Heaven and the new Earth. He becomes, in fact, the self-creating universe.

There comes a time for all of us to understand that only by being in harmony with the Divine Principle can we exist with order in a chaotic world of disorder. Since everything is linked to everything else, when we are out of harmony we are in the wilderness. We learn that everything is in a flow of perpetual movement. We can go with the tide and not fight against it. We start to realize that the only way we can really know this tide is through our own work in conscious awareness. We discover, paradoxically, that by being still we flow with the tide, in harmony, where we can learn the truths that underlie our existence on this planet. Only by being still and aware can we ever hear the voice inside each of us that can guide us on the way. Only by being still, and then learning, can we ever hope to move on to greater degrees of understanding. A teacher can point the way, and a mass of information can be poured down our throats, but only when we can reach some degree of harmony within ourselves can true knowledge be given.

It is as though we are birds flying in the wind. We are released from our cage and we fly upwards like the racing pigeon to try to find the way we must travel. Like the pigeon, we circle and circle, and the wind pushes us this way and that. Suddenly we feel we know the way we must go. We know we have a job to do, so we align ourselves in that direction and find our way to the other end. What makes it difficult for us is the mass of pre-conceived ideas and negative thinking that holds us down. We may sense the way, but the past, or fear, or laziness, or one of the many other failings we may have, drags us back to our false sense of "security." We are afraid to come into harmony with the Divine Principle that lies in each of us. The battle commences—the battle between the Principle and ourselves; it becomes a hard road, but we can learn to die every day, to let go of that which holds us back from understanding. Only by dying can we be reborn.

Harmony requires a fine degree of balance. There is the first axiom of "As above, so below." It is this balance that will allow the integration and assimilation of the congenial aspects of ourselves and attune us to what is given to us from our surroundings.

T HE FIXING OF GOLD IN THE HEART *"It is through this inner transformation, which is called 'the fixing of gold in the heart,' that any real change can come about."*

Alchemy is an art. It is a spiritual art form which, on its highest level, may bring about the complete transformation of man, both in this world and the next. At its lowest, it is a poor form of science or experiment, which is destined only to work with our lower natures and to feed man's ego without transformation.

What little we can know about alchemy on the surface comes through what we can study in books and engravings. There are smatterings of knowledge here and there, and indeed there are still existing today one or two real schools of alchemy, but these schools are always kept very secret. For reasons that are fairly obvious the pupils keep to themselves and don't discuss their training.

In such schools it is true that the object of the exercise is to produce gold in its physical form, but at the same time, the pupil is undergoing the inner transformation that enables the gold to be made in the last step of the opus. It is the inner transformation that I wish to describe. If there is to be a new age, a golden age, it is through this inner transformation, which is called "the fixing of gold in the heart," that any real change can come about.

In the process of alchemy, whether it be the alchemy of the inner man or the alchemy that is manifested in the outer world, it is necessary first to discover what it is that we are working with: What are the materials at hand, and what is their particular function? It is through observing what we have at hand that we can begin the task to which we have given ourselves.

The second step, working simultaneously with the first, is to ask ourselves, very deeply within, whether we are actually willing to sacrifice absolutely everything to complete the opus, and whether, by completing the opus, we will be more able to be of service.

Even though we may realize that this body is the only vehicle we have, we may or may not yet realize that this is the only time we have and that this is the only day there is. When we can come to accept this, we will realize that everything we need for the work to commence is already here.

In alchemy it is stated that whenever we define the space for which we are responsible, everything is given to us within that space. It is almost as if the whole universe comes down and sits at our feet, ready and waiting to be used to help the fulfillment of God's plan on Earth.

Man, at that moment, is no more the microcosm, but stands at the threshold of the greatest miracle of all—that God made man in His image. Man is the macrocosm, not the microcosm that he thought himself to be.

We have this vehicle or body, sometimes known as the temple of God, which is a most extraordinary miracle in itself. The brain is the most advanced computer ever known; oceans run in the veins; the mother's womb contains the future of the world in potential. The mineral kingdom can be found in the bodily trace elements. The vegetable kingdom, distilled many times, is within. The animal kingdom (with which we so often identify) is also within, either to work for us, or, at its worst, to destroy us before the Great Work is completed.

Within us also is a pearl of great price, the embryonic soul or essence of man—a dimensionless point, yet containing within it all dimension. The white rose is there within us; the red rose is within us; the gold is already there. In order to make gold in alchemy, we have to already have some gold before we start. Everything is there for the process to begin—the tools, the furnace, the crucible, and the vibration that is necessary to change the pattern of the material.

B ARRIERS TO TRANSFORMATION *"It is our degree of resentment, envy, or pride that prevents the transformation process from taking place."*

What is it that prevents us from completing, perhaps even starting, the work? There is something that prevents us, otherwise we would all be master alchemists and completely conscious beings.

Why is it that we can go to so many teachers and schools, and despite our good will, we are unable to complete even the early stages of the work? Is good will enough?

Just as it is necessary to see all the tools and materials that are made available to us when we set out on the journey, so it is also necessary to recognize what it is that prevents the experiment from taking place. That is the hard task with which we are faced. If we are strictly honest with ourselves and wish to set out on this journey, we will be able to see the stumbling blocks.

In our tradition, it is said that it is our degree of resentment, envy, or pride that prevents the transformation process from taking place. Somewhere we all know this, but for most of us it is also necessary that we are told these things. This is to confirm that inner suspicion that perhaps we are not yet ready to set out on the journey to the Soul, to Truth, until we have worked on the transformation and transmutation of the *nafs,* or animal soul. NOBODY CAN DO IT FOR US BUT OURSELVES!

We can be helped along the journey; we may be lucky enough to find a good guide who will do his or her best to keep us headed straight to our goal. Yet this inner work, which can be seen to be the minor opus of the great work, can only be done by ourselves.

Let us explore the nature of these three barriers, resentment, envy, and pride, which produce the sensations we feel so often—the sensations of apathy, grief, fear, and anger, none of which are attributes of God.

First, let us look at resentment. How many of us can say that we have no resentment? We are just ordinary human beings. We would not be human if we did not have some of this stuff of resentment. But we would be less than human if we did not recognize our failings and, in loving agreement with God, do our best to help them be transformed.

Basically, we resent the things we cannot change—matters which are usually rooted in the so-called past. Since in reality there is no past and no future, and since the object of the journey, the work, is to find the world of reality, we can also see that resentment cannot be an attribute of God, any more than apathy, grief, fear, or anger can be. We resent a sense of rejection that we may have experienced from our parents or friends. We resent the stupidity of the world, and of our fellow men, yet we do little to change that which lies within, which, finally, will change that which is seen to be without.

Resentment is a wall that cannot be climbed over. It is guarded by fierce animals, and there is a moat around the edge of the wall that is filled with danger. Whichever way we try to traverse this wall, we will find that there is no escape. Somehow we have to discover a completely new approach so that, one day, God willing, we will wake up to find that the wall is no longer there. The animals, instead of guarding the wall with their lives, are now quietly playing in the sunlight and have become our friends. The moat, before stagnant and filled with danger, has turned into a river that flows continuously towards the Great Ocean.

Now what about envy? Can we say that there is nothing

that we do not envy? Perhaps we have gotten over envying other's possessions, or their jobs, or their friends. Perhaps we are happy to accept things just as they are in the world around us. But how many of us can be clear enough to be able to say that we do not, in some psychic or spiritual manner, envy other's experiences?

I wonder how many times we may have been lying in bed or in contemplation in our own inner hunger, and yearned for the experience of a great teacher or mystic who had perhaps achieved the ultimate steps in the work. Envy is another great wall that cannot be traversed. It is as high and as dangerous as the first wall. If we do not recognize it, then we become more and more greedy, either for things in this world, or things in the other world. Eventually it can lead us to a sort of "spiritual nymphomania"—which can never be satisfied.

They say "pride goes before a fall." In the work, pride is the fall from God's grace. Pride is thinking that we alone can do something about things. Pride separates us from the First Cause. Pride makes us shunned by God.

Pride prevents us from truly giving anything. Rather, it makes us believe that we alone are the high and mighty, and that we can do something by ourselves. It prevents real change from taking place. Pride stops God from helping us in this process of inner transformation.

"Pride goes before a fall," the fall from grace that surely we have experienced so many times. It is indeed very painful. Although we may pick ourselves up and attempt to continue with the work, if the wall of pride is still there, the experiment will be ruined.

So what is the key that we need here? What is the key that will bring about real change within ourselves, and then in the outer world which so desperately needs change? The key is recognition. If we learn to recognize these barriers in ourselves with honesty and awareness—knowing that just as we long to know God, His own yearning is to be known—then these three walls of resentment, envy and pride will, little by little, fall away.

The key is recognition. If we accept this key willingly,

knowing that we can only be of service to God and mankind as these walls come down, then we will use the key. Little by little we will see that we can rise above the pain of apathy, grief, fear, and anger and discover that anger is transmuted into right motive and intention, apathy into flow, grief and self-pity into joy, and fear into ecstasy.

BEGINNING THE WORK *"For every act of surrender there is a release of energy, and thus a beginning of the work for which we were intended."*

It is man's responsibility to work on himself so that certain latent qualities lying dormant within him can be awakened, thus enabling him to be of real service to God and humanity for the reciprocal maintenance of the planet. In fact, the key to all is the word "service." Unless we put ourselves on the path of service we are not able to fulfill our obligations. There will be only the final and ultimate disappointment when we come to realize that our lives have been wasted in pursuing a goal "out there," some sort of illusion about developing the self that we have yet to discover, whereas what we are is the very goal for which we search. The "path of honesty" which in the Kabalistic tree of life is that straight way that leads from *Yesod,* the foundation, to *Tiphereth,* the heart center, the essential self, is the path of service and self-sacrifice. In it we give up all the opinions and concepts about ourselves that we have held so dear and which seem to give us a *raison d'etre* in this world.

On the surface, therefore, it is not a very promising picture. We seem to have put ourselves into such a position that unless there is a really great breakthrough in the consciousness of average man, it may be too late for anything to be done. Pollution, whether it is in the lakes or the oceans, on the land, or in the minds of men, takes certain very definite leaps and jumps. We can pour refuse into a lake for ages without too much ill effect, and then, quite suddenly, it is too late. After a flash-point everything that can support life dies and that, as they say, is that.

However, the very crisis that we have brought upon ourselves is at last awakening in us the needful desire to cooperate with each other. We need to cooperate with the different groups and centers that are springing up all around the planet, and thus with the invisible worlds. The all-pervading life in space is waiting to be awakened through recognition so that it can lead us back to our roots and to the knowledge that we need to put our planet back into order. Everywhere more and more ancient knowledge is being brought to the surface. Now is the time to build a system of interconnecting lines of force through the knowledge of the different types of energy. Man has the ability to transform these energies by working on himself so that he does truly become the link between Heaven and Earth, fulfilling the very function that was intended for him to fulfill on this planet.

In the so often misunderstood meaning of the "development of self," or "expansion of consciousness" (who is expanding what, I might ask!), it is very hard for us to keep ourselves clear of ultra-selfish motives. The ego has a way of becoming more and more subtle as we proceed along the path. We can fall into the trap of encapsulating the false "I" with concepts about this and that, about God, about the self. After all, it is only thought that divides us. In the beginning we were just "a thought in the mind of God." To come to understand how the creative principle works through the fourteen stages of thought, it is necessary to give up those concepts that have separated us from the truth for so long.

In the path of service, we enter the way of surrender. For every act of surrender there is a release of energy, and thus a beginning of the work for which we were intended. Mr. Gurdjieff would describe man as a "cosmic apparatus for the transformation of subtle energies." This implies that it is necessary to have the knowledge of both the apparatus and the energy it is intended to transform. In the path of service we give up our concepts in order to know who and what we are so that we can be truly conscious. Perhaps it could be said that man fulfills his obligation through recognition, redemption, and resurrection. It is only through re-cognition ("re-"

because in reality man has never been separated from the Light of Pure Intelligence) that we can be free and thus free others. When we recognize who and what we are, there is the redemption of the invisible kingdom, which, like everything else, wishes to return, once more, to the Light, to God. Return can only be through man—through the perfected man who has come to know and love God perfectly. From recognition and redemption comes the resurrection, or the birth of the real "I." The complete alchemical process has been fulfilled. There has been the passing away of all illusion of man's separateness, and there remains only the Truth itself.

TRANSFORMATION OF ENERGIES *"Certain transformations of energy come about which can then be used consciously for the reciprocal maintenance of the planet."*

It is not necessary to go into lengthy explanations about the transformation of energies. Rather let us concentrate on three aspects of transformation and explore them at some length.

The first of these comes about through man's own doing, through work on himself, and through accepting the exercises and disciplines that different teachers and schools give pupils to suit their particular needs. This work through one's own doing is very much involved with the "moving center" in man, or if you study the systems involving *chakras,* it is work on the base three centers.

The mineral kingdom sounds the note "do" of the octave, the vegetable kingdom, the "do" and the "re," and the animal the "do," the "re," and the "mi." Working on these centers allows us to cross the threshold, or "mi/fa" interval, and come upon the "heart center." The heart center is the seat of the essential self and the center of magnetism in man. The moving center is the focal point of electrical energy. The linking of these two centers with the "head center," or "thinking center," activated by the transformed energies of lower man, brings about the possibility of directed electro-magnetic force through the fusion of the male and female elements in man. We could put it this way: the mind, whether seen as Universal Mind or the mind given individuation through the affirmation of the "I" of man, participates in, and therefore uses, electrical energy. The spirit, illuminating the heart of man, gives rise to the latent magnetic force within him. If we do not work on ourselves in the moving center so that the false ego becomes dissolved through the note "fa"— or the fire of love, as the Sufis would put it—then we only spiritualize the false ego. This could create tremendous power and magnetism, bringing with it all sorts of supernatural experiences. Yet these powers are no evidence whatsoever of Divinity. It is only by sacrificing our little will to the Divine Will that we can be free and thus free others.

To do work on these first three notes of the octave it is necessary to build in the "observer." We have to learn so to observe the workings of our lower nature that we can come to recognize the pattern that is being produced in us all the time and thus bring about the necessary change. As I said before, it is through recognition that there is redemption. There comes a time when we feel the floodgates open. There is that great surge of joy that comes about when an aspect of us surrenders, and there is an immediate transformation of the energies involved.

I remember the first teacher I had when I was ten years old. He was the gamekeeper on my parent's estate in England. He taught me to catch rabbits with my bare hands by so watching and observing the movements of the rabbit that I came to be able to think like the rabbit; and more than this, to be able to anticipate what it would do before it knew what movement it was going to make. Finally, after my training period was over, I was told to kill the rabbit that I had caught with my hands. During that time I had studied so carefully the habits of the rabbit, I had come to love the animal kingdom so dearly, that the thought of killing the rabbit squirming in my hands was obviously abhorrent. Yet as the rabbit died, I knew then, as a boy, about redemption. At that exact moment there was such a flow of love that no words could ever express the feeling that came about.

If we could relate this to our daily lives, whether by being conscious about the transformation of the mineral and vegetable kingdom when we are eating our food or, after awakening the observer, by seeing what happens when the different aspects of the lower nature of man "die" through the light of recognition, then I believe we would come to realize what happens through the transformation of one aspect of energy to another aspect of energy. That boundless energy comes about because, through recognition there is redemption, and from redemption there is the resurrection of those different parts of the kingdom, those different energies, to give birth to the creation of a new "Earth." "For the old Heaven and the old Earth are passed away."

Although there are numerous books and pamphlets written on exercises that we can do to help us towards this transformation, and many groups and schools that are passing on the methods that they have found best for themselves, it would not be wrong, I feel, to give just a few simple pointers as to how work can be done on this first aspect of the transformation of energy. In the moving center we are dealing with the world of *Maya* (appearances), the world of time, the influence of the moon, the false notion of change, and therefore the desire of the ego to attempt to alter that which is, in essence, perfect. We are dealing with the world of phenomena, be they physical, emotional, or psychic. We are dealing with the world of experience—"me" experiencing this or that, or even going so far as to think that "I" could cause something which would bring about some sort of altered state of consciousness. Work on the moving center has a very specific function that has to do with the word "preparation." It does not matter whether the method we use is *Hatha Yoga,* or *Tai Chi,* or other exercises from the different traditions, it is still only a preparatory stage. We are preparing that center to work for us rather than against us (even to enjoy working for us!). For this to happen, we have to break the incessant clock, stamp on it, and throw away the pieces.

The moving center is dependent on the false notion of time, and therefore on the false notion of space. It even creates time in order to continue the illusion of its own existence as separate from others. If we have two moving centers trying to communicate with each other we have one illusion trying to pass on that illusion to another illusion! There is no real change, which must come about through proper communication. There is just the apparency of change. For work on this center, we need to allow the past to be burnt in the present moment. By observing continuously the games that are being played, we come to the eventual recognition of the superiority of the observer, and the willingness on the part of the many beings within that center to be redeemed and transformed into another, higher form of energy. But it is a long struggle! It is not as though the transformation of these aspects can be achieved overnight. It is a continuous battle with the illusions, the fears, the grief, the greed and the apathy that arise within.

The second type of transformation of energy comes about not from one's own doing, or from work on oneself through exercises, breathing practices, movements, etc., but from the art of surrender. Surrender is an art for it requires great courage, and indeed will-power, to be able continuously to surrender to a higher force. In the first instance, in the preparatory work, we managed to start to get control over our lower nature through recognition. On the way we were given many signs that we were on the right path. Joy sprang up in our heart each time that the lower energies were brought over the threshold of individuated consciousness, and, slowly but surely, a magnetic center was formed to which others would come to share in the way. We lost the sense of "I"ness that held us back and realized that perhaps the quality that the moving center had to achieve was patience— the hardest thing for this world involved with time and space and movement cycles. In the feeling center of the heart we have to learn humility, and that comes about through conscious surrender and self-sacrifice, sometimes described as "conscious suffering."

Let me try to put it simply in the light of what has already been said. The lower, or moving center, has very much to do with the nature of electrical energy. A thought is an electrical impulse. In our unenlightened state, it is not difficult to come to realize that it is thought that separates us. The moment those thoughts are transformed through the heart we come to meet each other. There is no more separation; there is attraction through magnetism rather than the false attraction that existed before. In that false attraction, we felt drawn to one another or to a group, but in fact what we wanted to do was to change the other.

The "I" can rest, for it discovers the humility that comes about through knowledge of the self, and realizes that there is just one Cause, one law that pervades and permeates all life. The preparatory work that was done in the moving center brings man to the first stage of realization. He has found, for the first time, his individuated soul, an electromagnetic force field which has no beginning and no end, no before and no after. He is now given power over the elements that made up the lower energies which, in turn, precipitated his physical body and the world of material substance.

Perhaps we can now see how there are two very different approaches to the necessary transformation of energy, dependent upon whether we are doing work on the moving center, or work involved with the feeling center. In the first instance, we are required to make conscious efforts to "break the clock," the cyclical patterns, so that we can escape from the tyranny of our conditioned minds. In the second instance, we have to learn the art of surrender to the Higher Force so that, little by little, certain transformations of energy come about which can then be used consciously for the reciprocal maintenance of the planet.

In the third type of transformation, there is nothing more that "we" can do about it. This transformation occurs solely through Divine Grace, and whatever we do, whatever realization we may have come to, we never know if or when this will be given to us. It comes like a lightning flash in the darkness of human ignorance. It instantaneously transforms even the new "I" that has emerged, like the Phoenix, from the ashes of the old, and joins it forever with the one Source of all life, giving the knowledge of the act of creation stretched out through time

B EING AND CAPACITY *"Only when we are in the present moment can there be the empty center demanding nothing for itself."*

The Work, sometimes called the Spirit of God, is not something that we can "do," but rather something which we can more or less consciously participate in. First of all, that means we must be awake.

So many people being born into the spritual renaissance of our time feel that they have something to do, some special mission or other to fulfill. They forget the necessary functions of life. The functions I am referring to here involve the very basic activities of our lives, such as eating, gardening, carpentry, business work, and so on. These functions are vitally necessary, that the Spirit of God may manifest itself on the relative plane. A gardener is no more important than a spiritual teacher, and vice versa, in the overall picture of life. A mountain is no more important than a tree, nor a river more important than a lake. Everything fits together in a perfect pattern, if we can only see it. I am sure we all know that some of the wisest people we meet are the simple people, living simple lives on the land, helping to manifest the Will of God. Will and Spirit are like two hands on the same body in what we call the reciprocal maintenance of the planet.

The spiritual work is not glamorous, although we can believe that it is; it is hard work on whatever level it is done. In whichever of the three circles the work manifests itself, there is a necessary function within the overall plan.

To come to the esoteric circle, there are steps along the way which start with this word we call "function." That is why in the old days, people were not brought into the inner teachings until they were around 40 years old, by which time they should have been able to get their physical world together, become householders and be responsible for the environment in which they lived. Today times have changed, but the circles existing within the work are just as important now as they always have been, and always will be, until the new age is really with us. In fact, I would go further and say that the new age is dependent, to a very great extent, upon our understanding of these things.

So often we want to jump into the esoteric circle with all good heart and will, and yet we have not yet become apprentices of daily life. The result is that, although we may be granted a taste of what lies beyond the boundaries of the human mind, and indeed beyond consciousness itself, we become bitterly disappointed, for we fail to be able to live a normal everyday life. Thus, we have to start all over again.

The outer circle, through which we may proceed towards the center, the core of the work, must not exist only as a stepping stone to true freedom. At the same time, the process is going both ways, so that, as I said before, each step is dependent upon the other. The esoteric circle is totally dependent upon the exoteric for its survival—and here I mean the bringing of the Kingdom of Heaven on Earth, as in the Lord's Prayer.

Now, what about the mesoteric path? What is it that stands between the so-called outer and so-called inner worlds? It would seem that it stands almost like a bridge. Let me put it as clearly as I can, although it takes a long time in our world for the second step to be truly a bridge, for us to be truly ready. The mesoteric circle has to do with the word "being." Being has to do with capacity, and paradoxically enough, capacity has to do with emptiness. Being is like a chalice. It would be helpful if we used an analogy here. Consider the Mass in the Christian Church—and there are very similar rituals in certain dervish orders as well. First of all, the chalice must be made of the finest material, perfectly shaped by a craftsman who has undergone many years of training so that his craft may become an image of God's perfection. We might see this work as being part of function, although of course in the old days, those who made such beautiful objects were initiates of the highest degree. The chalice is kept in a special place, always clean and always ready for the moment of the Mass. The priest, at the right time, takes the chalice, fills it with the wine of the Holy Sacrament, and, having taken a little himself first, gives it to those who are ready to receive it. At the end of the ceremony, any wine that has not been received is not allowed to be left. The priest himself completes the cycle.

We are moving into the recognizing of the mesoteric stage of the work. I am also referring to the work in general, the work that is intended to help bring about the necessary changes on our planet. The form of the chalice is created so that the empty space within the shape or form may be a receptacle for the Spirit.

Now, as I said, being and capacity go together. If we are not in the present moment, but are always either in the past (through the degree of our conditioning, our envy, resentment or pride) or else projecting into the future, there is no being. There is merely the running away of the mind—like some wild horse, which, however wonderful, is only useful when it is trained to fulfill its true function. Here we come back to function once more, for there is a function in everything we see or feel or hear in the relative world. But the function has to be known and understood, that it may become useful. When the horse stands still, we can mount the horse. If it is galloping, we will never catch it.

Only when we are in the present moment can there be the empty center demanding nothing for itself. As I said before, this takes time, for it takes time for conditioning to be cleared in the relative sense. It takes time to cease to be spiritually ambitious. It takes time to learn to be.

Did not Jesus once say, "Be with me as I am with you always"? These are perhaps not the exact words, but they express some of the inner meaning of being. Here I ask that we read between the lines of everything I say, for words are only vehicles to carry the truth, although they do, indeed, carry action within them. Being is not something we can achieve alone. That is why it is necessary for there to be a group.

Being comes about through sacrifice and surrender, the sacrifice of who and what we think we are, that the alchemical process of transformation may take place. Imagine a circle of friends, all sacrificing their illusions to the center. The center is a fire, but it is the fire of love to which we aspire. From the ashes the chalice is built, the vehicle that can contain the Spirit. The Spirit cannot be contained in any of our illusions of self-importance—the illusions created by the grinding clash of opposites that make us feel we ought to be something. The chalice is made from our longing and yearning to know the truth, that we might be of service. The High Mass is the great act of service, for, from the transmutation of wine into Spirit, those coming to receive that Holy Sacrament may have their hearts spiritualized. The great danger is always that, as *baraka* flows, the ego may be spiritualized rather than the heart.

We may see now why real knowledge is necessary, why this journey is not a sentimental and glamorous path, and perhaps why it can be said to be a path of love, compassion and service. We want to serve. We want nothing else. What could it mean to serve? Is it not to be capable of the greatest act of service in this world, to be able to be a vehicle for the Spirit of God? Is not the Aquarian Age symbolized by the overflowing of the chalice onto the earth?

Let no one be so proud that he or she cannot chop wood, clean houses, make a garden, etc. At the same time, let us understand that these functions to which I have referred are all part of the work and may be done more or less consciously by each one of us. This is first of all dependent upon our willingness to learn, to be of service, and the amount of attention we give to it.

Let us consider the analogy of the bee. Most people think, "How wonderful; bees make honey," but they seldom contemplate them as part of the glory and beauty of God. We seldom really contemplate the glory and beauty of God to the degree we should. It is indeed a miracle that bees make honey, that there are different flavors and colors, and that it is still all honey. It is not so often considered that there is a second miracle to the bee. Not only is one substance formed through the transformation of subtle energies in the bee, but they also form another substance in which they make their own house. And that is quite a miracle. If we go a bit further, we discover that the house is made in a hexagonal form. And the reason for this is that the hexagonal form is the right shape for the bee.

The third thing the bee does is that it cross-pollinates the plants. We forget what this can mean because we look at the forms in the world and we do not see the real world. What is this telling us of the real world? If we are human beings we should at least be up to the level of a bee. Are we? One day I realized that I was not, and that is what made me begin to study. I was not even able to be conscious or awake enough to fulfill my function as a being. A bee does it unconsciously or instinctively. But man should be able to be a conscious apparatus for the transformation of subtle energies and thereby produce at least honey, or what that might mean. He should also be able to produce the substance to build his own house, and the shape, too. And he should be able to realize that, in knowledge, he is cross-pollinating.

When we came here, we brought something, and when we go, we will take something of this place. If we knew what this was, we would know it is a substance. It is produced through us through transformation, through work on ourselves, and it is absolutely limitless. This substance defines areas and makes shapes. There are people in the world who have the knowledge to be able to produce that substance.

Chalice Prayer

Father, to Thee I raise my whole being, a vessel emptied of self.
Accept, Lord, this my emptiness, and so fill me with Thyself,
Thy light, Thy love, Thy life, that these, Thy precious gifts,
May radiate through me and overflow the chalice of my heart
Into the hearts of all whom I may contact this day,
Revealing unto them the beauty of Thy joy and wholeness,
And the serenity of Thy peace, which nothing can destroy.

PATTERN *"Remember that the needs of a person relate to the pattern of his life, in relationship to those around him and to the environment itself."*

People tend to forget the interconnectedness of all things, both visible and invisible, tangible and intangible. It is still almost impossible for people to understand the words of the great English mystic Thomas Thaherne: "You cannot pick a flower without the troubling of a star." In modern science, the realization of the interconnected patterns of our life is emerging with greater acceleration than ever before. Unfortunately, that does not mean to say that this realization has increased our sensitivity to these interconnected patterns.

One of the tasks before us today is to work on ourselves within *le dedans des choses* (the "within-ness" of things) to enhance the degree of our sensitivity until we may actually see and know how to make a better world in harmony. It is almost our obligation to become more sensitive. We may then find that our attitude towards life takes on a radical change, and sometimes quite quickly. We can be sensitive to the needs of others. We can make ourselves available to be more of service to this planet, to the different kingdoms therein, and the different "worlds" that exist all the time with our own.

Remember that the needs of a person relate to the pattern of his life, in relationship to those around him and to the environment itself. I'm sure we all remember the saying, "The road to Hell is paved with good intentions." We can create Hell for other people with all the goodwill of our concept of the world, without the sensitivity and knowledge to note the real need in the moment. Nothing can happen until the time is right. The ability to be sensitive to others and to their needs is an art emanating from love itself, anchored in knowledge of everything from psychology to the understanding of time in its many dimensions.

We can become sensitive to the various kingdoms of nature: the mineral kingdom, the vegetable kingdom, the animal kingdom, and mankind. It is unnecessary to describe our usual insensitivity to these kingdoms which support our lives in this world. Many of us feel despair about man's greed and ignorance and lack of respect for ecology. Some of us are noticing the implications of our own insensitivity.

Let us remember that whatever is found in this world is indeed only an apparency of the real world. We need to become sensitive to the real world. It is the real world that creates the apparency, and not the other way around. It is ideas that produce change. As was once said by Hadji Bairam Wali, a great Sufi mystic and saint, "There is no creation in the relative world, there is only the becoming of Being."

Man is the link between Heaven and Earth. Therefore, he has the responsibility of fulfilling God's plan for the Earth. He must learn to BE. When he knows without any shadow of a doubt that there is just one absolute Being, he can learn to participate consciously in the transformations of energy. An animal has only two sections of brain, but man has a "thinking" brain as well. Therefore, man has an extra responsibility, beyond that of his animal nature.

The Druids knew the responsibility of man, and were able to contribute consciously to what G. I. Gurdjieff called "the reciprocal maintenance of the planet." They knew how to work with the interconnected lines of force which comprise the etheric body of the Earth. The standing stones at Stonehenge were not placed there arbitrarily because it was nice countryside, nor were they there just for witnessing the rising of the sun over a special stone at the summer equinox. They were placed there in a special formation, in exact proportions which correspond to and reflect the interconnected patterns of "ley" lines and power points found in the etheric system of England and the world. The stones act as giant acupuncture needles to help harmonize the natural energies.

After working with the Arch-Druid of his time, some twenty years ago, I studied these energy flows using the techniques of dowsing (often used to find water or minerals), and I saw that the time was ripe to bring back this ancient knowledge for the healing of the planet. In the old days (and by the way, it is still done in China today) houses would seldom be built until the owner and the builder had called in someone skilled in the art of geomancy.

A geomancer is someone who knows about the invisible world, the all-pervading life in space, and who is able to advise people on the best place to locate a house, and where the different rooms should be situated. He understands ley-lines, and knows the right trees and herbs to plant in the right positions to blend with the energies of the people and the site. Thus the geomancer helps to align and harmonize the various kingdoms, enabling the inhabitants to better maintain the flow of energies between themselves and the land for which they are custodians.

This knowledge has not been lost! The natural lines, even though they may have been blocked by cities or highways, can be worked with and made active again. One stream can meet and join with another stream that has lain dormant for hundreds of years. Man once more can develop the skills lying dormant within him, so that he can put the planet back into order. This can happen only if he cares enough, if he can see beyond the veils of his limited ego-consciousness and can devote himself to a life of service to God and mankind.

I am offering some ideas that can change our attitude to our lives and to those around us. We are dealing with pattern and with a living force that is readily available to us if we truly love and respect nature. We are talking about the establishing of shapes and designs in this world which carry the order and harmony of the higher worlds. We are attempting to act as a bridge, ourselves, between Heaven and Earth.

It is through language that the pattern, or blueprint, of a culture may manifest itself. It is pattern that we are looking at, in whatever way it is manifested, be it in design, be it in architecture, be it in what is called "the shape of things to come."

It is not possible even to think of a word without producing a subtle sound in our consciousness. In some very strange way we may even have a memory pattern of all sounds. For example, if we use the word "projection," it may be possible for the mind to recall the archetypal sound of the word. A pattern will be set up which will be held there in suspension as long as the sound continues.

Now the origin of pattern is not a series of lines, or even a line. What is it? This is the point of it all, the one point. If I draw a pattern, it can be understood to have originated from a dot. Once more I would like to stress that all we are seeing is the manifestation of another, invisible pattern. In the same way that each line has a relationship corresponding to the others, so the invisible pattern has relationship.

The dot can be seen to represent a dimensionless point. As we see it, there is no real dimension, and what we actually see is merely a representation of what cannot be seen, let alone talked about. Yet something has to be seen here, in this world to act as a challenge, a guideline to the real world.

Now a dimensionless point actually contains all dimension within it. It is there, latent. It is a world of possibilities. Nothing has happened, there is no creation, and yet there is all possibility of creation. This point is literally a substance. It exists in the fifth dimension, beyond time and space as we know it, containing everything. Yet nothing, so far, has happened.

What we are looking at here is that beyond, or through, the fourth dimension of time, there is another "dimension"— although that is hardly a fair word in this context—in which or interpenetrating which there is a complete world of possibility, not having dimension as we know it with the senses, yet containing dimension and the world of time.

Thus, if the pattern is merely a representation of an invisible pattern, so the dot is just a representation as well. This dot is a substance, and from this substance all the possibilities of the matrix can be drawn across the face of the earth. It exists in a state of randomness. Perhaps now it can be seen that by entering in the path of service, real service, it is possible that the pattern for our children's children may be brought forth through us.

It is man who can be a double instrument, within unity. If we can accept that every pattern has a sound and if we can see that every sound produces a pattern, then there is the possibility of something in man that can link these two aspects, bringing them together.

What is this quality that man alone has? It is not contained in the mineral world; it is not contained in the vegetable world, nor even in the animal world, but it is contained in man. It is conscious will. This is the key that we need to look at, for without conscious will, man can do nothing. He can sound a note, creating a pattern that may or may not be useful, and he can manifest God's own uniqueness in himself, with or without the Original Sound being heard. Without conscious will he is a half-hearted creature. With will he can act as a link between Heaven and Earth. It is through man that the sound, the energy, can be harnessed for good.

Throughout the world there are very definite power points where *chi,* or life force, gathers. In geomancy these are called "caves," and they act as wombs. The immediacy of the living *chi,* for which there is no substitute, is the final seal of validity in geomancy; it supercedes all the detailed techniques and scholastic knowledge. As it is said, "All the multifarious methods were devised for no other purpose than to seek out the living *chi.*" When the living *chi* is found, there is no longer the least need to discuss methods. If we come upon this life force, whatever name we give to it, we do not need methods.

The work is very much connected with coming upon this *chi,* not, I repeat, *not* through a concept of personal development, but through an act of self-surrender and sacrifice. All methods come about, as Plato said, "when knowledge is dying and a new form of knowledge is necessary." Yet the methods are useful only to bring us to find this ever living force, which is neither "within" nor "without" but which interpenetrates all life. Call it what you will, it is there. If we come upon it as human beings, we have free choice as to how to use it—for our own ends, for the benefit of a small group of people, or for conscious evolution and humanity as a whole.

We can go through the fourth dimension of time into the infinite world of possibilities. It is through man, perfected man, that the world of possibilities can manifest here on Earth. It is our obligation to become complete, so that we ourselves are the bridge.

As it is so aptly described in the *Upanishads,* "There is

something so small that you cannot see it, so great that you cannot describe it, and this is *Atman,* the pure Spirit. There is a bridge between Heaven and Earth. This is *Atman.*" When we have given up all notions of ourselves, who and what we think we are, we are the manifestation of the bridge, the Spirit, and there is no separation. Essence needs form through which to manifest itself, and form needs Spirit to live.

COMMUNITY *"A vortex sets up a magnetic force field which inevitably attracts to itself those souls who are looking for the sort of way provided from such a place."*

At certain special times the formation of communities is made possible. If we look back in history we will see that this opportunity occurs following certain very definite cycles.

For example, around 700 years ago communities were set up to last for the next "age," or 700 years. These communities were vehicles for carrying certain knowledge through the times of crisis that were ahead. In those days there were the Christian communities, and of course, the dervish brotherhoods. These communities, particularly the Christian communities in Europe, were usually connected to an already existing village structure that had grown up over a very long period of time. Although the community was frequently found quite a way from the village, even if the community was a "closed order," there was still a very vital link with the life of the village.

The reason for this connection can be seen if we realize that there will always need to be an outer, a middle, and an inner aspect to the community itself. There are many reasons for this; we have discussed many of them in the past. There are many levels of understanding, and at this time, when the idea of community is so much in the air, it is wise to ponder these things very carefully.

If we believe in God, we trust in His perfection. That means that the patterns of the various communities that are destined to be built are already set in the formative worlds, with the possibility of manifesting themselves correctly in this world.

Each of the community centers that is being set up all over the world is coming into being because of need. Out of our mutual needs a community is born. Some are interested in natural farming, some in crafts. Some turn into intensive "schools" where men and women are trained to go back into the world to help link centers together in knowledge and love. Some are communities which come into being for a while and then disperse because it is not intended for them to stay. They act as "filters" that sift people out and then direct them to places where they will be really useful. There are some centers that are set up, based on natural law, to fulfill certain functions destined to anchor energy and knowledge for the next six hundred years.

One type of center is built on, or very near, a "power point." This is the most difficult type of center to run since any power point magnifies both the positive and the negative aspects of our characters and personalities. In such a center we can expect to find tremendous changes within individuals. Some people cannot stand the speed of the change. The power released in such a center is destined for certain purposes, but until the understanding of this is given we have to be very attuned, very in love with the Divine Purpose. Otherwise the elemental force released can turn back on us, angrily demanding recognition.

I remember such a case in England at one of the centers with which I had been involved. Tremendous energy was released. Each time we forgot God and our intention, we would be shocked into taking stock, once more, of the nature and purpose of our lives. On two occasions at that center when we forgot, a huge wind developed out of nowhere. Once it blew in a great fourteen foot window, roared around the dome, and then disappeared. On another occasion it made a vortex in the grounds, snapping two great trees as though they were matchsticks. Beware of power without knowledge and love!

Those who have offered up their lives, and the concepts and opinions about their lives, in service to God and humanity, will be given the knowledge of what is necessary. Knowledge is given, not acquired, but it can only be given at the right time. Many people are convinced that now is the time for people of good will to build communities that will establish the etheric web of light around the globe.

Through the recognition of the growth of group consciousness we can go beyond the boundaries of our limited ego-consciousness and begin to touch on the responsibility of being man and woman. When we are truly of service to the group and to the individuals within the group, and if we remain detached from our own personal aims and ambitions, then change can come about in our relationships which will have a very profound effect on the nature of the work with which we are involved. As long as we are still floundering about in the concept of "self-development" rather than in "self-surrender," the group is bound to take on a rigidity which, in the end, will lead to its disruption.

Personality problems and the like may lead us to forget our original intention. If the energy released through the group for the work of the reciprocal maintenance of the planet is misdirected, real growth becomes difficult. The object of the awakening of group consciousness is to provide the best possible circumstances for people to be together in order to empty themselves of their concepts, and so be filled with the Light of Pure Intelligence.

A vortex sets up a magnetic force field which inevitably attracts to itself those souls who are looking for the sort of way provided from such a place. Like attracts like, and a "spiritual family" is formed. Out of that family, partnerships are set up, smaller groups are formed, and mutual interests are shared. In every family there are bound to be personality problems, but there is mutual aim and understanding which can hold together the family even in the most difficult circumstances.

The first purpose is to establish this vortex or magnetic field. This, in a sense, is a being slowly being made ready for independent existence. In the early stages the being is as primitive and fragile as the most fragile parts of our own nature. It will move along the path of the agreement made by the group itself. In other words, it will move along a directed path. If the agreement of the group is towards love and openness, then that will be its direction. If the movement of the group is towards directing particular opinions or concepts towards an individual, or towards a particular method of approach, that being will move in that direction, adding power to the opinions of those people within the vortex itself.

The fragility of this being cannot be stressed enough. To use an analogy, for a long time the being of the vortex is hardly aware of its own existence in the relative world. For it to grow into itself, with its own individual and universal understanding of the nature of love and the path of service, it needs to be fed the right "food," the food of love and the sacrifice of the concept of ourselves as separate from the whole.

For anything we are given there is in turn an obligation to give something back. We are obliged, in return for all that we are given, to sacrifice ourselves towards the fulfillment of the dream. Only in that way can that being, the vortex, spin its way into independent existence, eventually becoming a guiding light and indeed the food for all those who come to it. There is another secret here, and that is that this being is divisible into as many parts as those who trust it. The light can be carried to any part of the world and placed on suitable ground, where it will grow in harmony with the original vortex that was set up at the beginning of the impulse. It is like taking a light from one candle. From that one light we can light as many candles as are waiting to be lit. It is easy to see how this applies to the highest—the Light of God.

Another purpose of the work is redemption. Redemption is much talked about in the Christian Church and in all esoteric work. Sadly, it is often forgotten that without recognition there can be no redemption. True recognition is the knowledge of the real self. Towards this end, or shall we call it this beginning, there are many stages which we can observe. When we learn to recognize the essence of a plant or a tree, then that tree "comes alive," grows more, gives back more to us as we give more to it through our recognition of it. When we learn to recognize and cooperate with the invisible king-doms, the invisible kingdoms, without which nothing can come to pass, cooperate with us.

The understanding of this law of reciprocity is vital for any real group work. Suffice it to say that for something to be born, something apparently has to die. Yet there is no death. If we substitute the word "redemption" for "death," we may come to understand that it is through recognition, the knowl-edge of the true self, that death is overcome once and for all. Instead of death there is continuous redemption and thus the continuing of life.

What is being redeemed? Let us take a simple analogy here. A group of people choose to come together once a week, in order to share knowledge and experience, to meditate, to pray, and so on. If the group is working correctly at all, then the individuals will know that it is not a question of taking from the group, but rather of giving to the center. "God has no needs, so give Him yours." As the individuals assemble together and , step by step, give up their tensions, their pain, their concepts, and their thoughts, those pains and opinions are redeemed. They are, in a sense, put into the melting pot, the cauldron, which the Chinese call the *ting*. If there is sufficient heat (and here, the heat I am referring to is the fervor or passion of love), then from that redemption some-thing new, that was not apparently there before, is born. This is the process of alchemy.

It does not matter what other things people do for their purification and development. It does not particularly matter what it is they study. What matters is the reason for being together and the degree of love that allows people to come together on a regular basis to help towards the fulfillment of the law of God. I believe that if we take a step now, we will be given all the proof, the outward and visible signs, to show us that we are moving in the right direction.

The need for group work and group cooperation is vital at this time of history. People go so far as to say that it is only through this work that a cataclysmic disaster in this world can be avoided.

It is so easy to see how things can go wrong if true balance is not functioning correctly. We can work conscientiously with the *kath* center or the *hara* center and become excellent at martial arts, and yet forget to pick up the garbage! Or we can study and study and be filled with all sorts of concepts, and yet have so little life force flowing through us that we are unable to get out of bed. We can even open up the heart in joy, and still run into a state of chaos—loving and feeling desperately about everything, yet unable either to stand still or to do something about it, to know why we are doing it or what we are doing. For true balance to exist it is surely essential that there be equal amounts of work on the thinking center, the feeling center, and the moving center. Where has all the music gone from our groups and the deep inner joy that is beyond happiness? If we discard all that is no longer necessary, I am sure we will come upon a format for group work which will satisfy, on as many levels as are necessary, the needs of those who come to us.

Now is the time to work together, to fulfill our obligation to life. Human life is supported by the continuous sacrifices of the mineral world, the vegetable world, and the animal world—the first three notes of the octave. We become human as we cross the threshold to be responsible at last, responding to the call that, if we could but listen and hear, is in every moment. We respond to the note "fa," sounding in the heart center, so that everything may return consciously to the One, as all is manifested from the One. To understand this redemption is the beginning of the "new age."

BROTHERHOOD *"If we do not consider the needs of another, we are considering ourselves alone."*

A spiritual community is not exempt from the problems of the world, because the spiritual community is part of, and living within, an over-all community. Mevlana Jelaluddin Rumi talks about the foam on top of the ocean, and how when the wind blows, the foam blows off and goes somewhere else.

At any one moment of time there is anger, fear and grief; there is apathy; there is logical tyranny. These exist all of the time. And like the foam, they are blown off the ocean, going somewhere. We are not yet complete human beings, over and through whom the foam blows and is taken back to its source. All of us are people who are doing our best to help bring about what we call a new world. So often we say, "I am angry" or "I am sad," or "You are angry" or "You are sad." The reality is not like that. There is anger, there is fear, there is grief, there is apathy, and there is tyranny. These will go on until the day of recognition, creating the very pressure that is needed for people to turn straight.

In a spiritual community, where we can really help each other to understand these things, we need very much to come into the knowledge that it is not totally our own anger, grief, or pain that exists within us. When we come together in community, everything is accelerated and dramatized. It becomes a real theater, a theater of life. Some of us are young and have not been in the spiritual work very long. Some of us have been around it quite a long time. Still, all of us have the same problem, an unattended situation. If we identify with something that is an unredeemed form of energy, we are not doing the work we are asked to do here. We are asked to participate in the work as consciously as we can. The work has nothing to do with anger, grief, fear, and tyranny; it has to do with the redemption of them, but not identification with them.

A community can never be based on personality. We are not allowed, in a community, to bounce off each other's problems. Many, many communities have started in the name of this or that, but few ever last. They do not last because they use this bounce-off technique to deal with individual pain or suffering, which just reinforces separation. They are terrified of coming into union. Are we not, all of us, equally terrified? If we are really honest about it, this is what we are frightened of; this is the ultimate fear. We are all terrified of coming to that point which is beyond that which we can speak about, beyond that which justifies what we think our existence is on

Earth; beyond what we think gives us some *raison d'etre!*

Spiritual community can exist only through non-identification, though this does not mean to say we ignore pain and suffering. Quite the reverse. Spiritual community is totally involved with the pain and suffering of the world, and yet not identified with it. The work of a spiritual community is beyond the mind, beyond consciousness, so that we cannot really talk about it. We can ask whether God is involved with pain and suffering. We can ask how this suffering can be alleviated. This is work for a spiritual community.

It is no longer helpful to follow a charismatic leader who owns people through spiritual tyranny. At times of history certain people have manifested a certain power, in God's name, to hold something together. If we are free ourselves, we may be able to help people who are trapped in their identification with their illusory convictions. Spiritual tyranny comes about when a leader uses other people to support his or her own quasi-convictions. The key to freedom is in a degree of realization beyond belief systems. Know that there is foam on the surface of the ocean; know it is blowing on the wind; and know that it will come and go.

Do not deny anger; do not deny fear; do not deny pain. Denying them will not do any good at all. Accept them as they are, and accept that they will go on until the end of time. That is the day of recognition, when we go beyond time.

In non-identification, the first word is always "Yes." We can be still and centered for a moment and say "Yes." Yes there is pain, yes there is anger, yes there is rejection, and yes it is so. It becomes acceptance and recognition of the pain of the world, without sentimentality or emotionality. There can be action, but action proceeds from acceptance and centering. We can extend this acceptance and recognition to every creature in the world.

Have we ever heard a plant scream when it is picked? If we pick it and are awake, it does not scream, but if we tear it from the ground, it screams. When we are not angry with, or reacting to, each other, we are in a state of being in which there is acceptance. This is coming together to return home.

I believe that the capacity for real brotherhood comes either from having experienced an immense amount of personal pain and sacrifice, or from discipline we received when we were children. Brotherhood does not happen by itself. We cannot presume we are brothers, nor can we assume there is brotherhood. It is to be worked for and striven for, in the understanding (if not, at least in the trust) that without brotherhood we do not fulfill God's love on Earth. Brotherhood is in love—in love with the one Divine Truth, the One, the First Cause of all creation. In that understanding, all personality, all masks, are melted in the Divine Love that grants us life.

If we do not consider the needs of another, we are considering ourselves alone. That is stupid, since we do not exist apart from the one divine principle. It could be said that we do not have an individual soul as yet, since until we realize we are a spark of the universal and divine flame, our concept of individuality is an illusion. But what is man? Where does consideration start? Did not God, who is beyond, before, and within all life, make man in His image? If we purport to love God, then the very early steps of the possibility of brotherhood start in consideration of love, for He, as it is said in Christian terms, brought Himself to earth manifested in man. For what possible reason would this be except that, first through consideration, and then through brotherhood, we may all come to love Him as He loves us?

Let us be considerate and truly learn about brotherhood. Live in brotherhood and we will become free.

Brotherhood is based upon need, a longing to cooperate in the knowledge and love of God, and in the realization that there is nothing else to do. There is no point in going back to an old order when we have to bring in a new order. It cannot be based upon personality; no true brotherhood can. If it is, it will fail, or become spiritual fascism. We are not important at all; we are part of a great and beautiful cosmic process, but we are not more important than the process. We certainly are not more important than God. As long as we think we are important, as long as we demand our happiness, as long as we demand our experience, emotionally, physically, spiritually, or any other way—as long as we demand anything—we are centered in that thing. If we are centered in anything by demanding it, we are stuck in ME, ME, ME, and we can never cross what they call in the *I Ching* "the great water." The great water is between "You" and "Me." So I say that no brotherhood can be based upon personality.

Also, remember we cannot work on "personality" with "personality." It is like trying to work on the ego with ego—all we get is thousand-headed serpents. We say in Sufism, "Love turns even copper into gold." Love will melt personality. Love will not destroy, but will melt, will redeem.

SERVING THE GUEST *"May I be allowed to be of service this day?"*

Brotherhood cannot be based upon fear, or greed, or bitterness, or resentment. If we are in a state of resentment, no longer wishing to serve our fellow human being (who surely can be the manifestation of the one Guest) then we will not be of service. Perhaps we will produce food that is not to our guest's liking, or we will forget that our guest might like some fresh flowers in his or her room, a smiling face to welcome him with, and a loving heart to receive him.

In reality there is only one Guest. Would the Guest wish to enter a place that is not clean? Would He wish to sleep on a bed that was not spotless? Would He wish to eat from a kitchen that did not sing with the divine light?

It is not difficult to understand the answer if we are truly honest with ourselves. After all, would we, as guests, wish to enter our friend's house, only to find that there was no clean towel, no soap in the basin, no clean bath where we could wash so that we could be good guests?

As custodians of a house, we have the privilege to serve the house and all those who enter its gates. We yearn to serve, and thus we find joy in keeping the house clean and full of His light, which cannot shine if dirt exists.

Dirt attracts psychic dirt, which attracts resentment. If we are dirty, we attract dirt. We wash that we can pray. We wash that we can truly make love, that we can be clear channels to serve God, the one and only Being. We cannot expect God to wash us, for He gives us the means to wash ourselves. We cannot even consider that one of the brotherhood would ever get close to us without our being clean. The first principle of any brotherhood or any healing work is cleanliness.

True healing comes from truth and returns to truth. Sometimes people are not well because they have allowed themselves to be caught in fate, and sometimes this can be deemed necessary. We must not judge. In true healing, there must be no judgment, no opinion. If we are open within the present moment, we can be allowed to experience what is necessary for the situation, be it work on the land, work on the vegetable or animal kingdoms, or work with mankind.

Healing has to do with an analysis of the situation, the person, and the true cause of the suffering. The questions to be asked are: "May I?", "Should I?" and "Can I?" "May I?" refers to permission from a higher source; "Should I?" has to do with the right thing at the right time; and "Can I?" relates to my own state of being and capacity.

Living in the question will produce the answer. Yes! But, by God, we have got to live in it and have the passion to live in it. Live in the question—go to bed with it; get up with it; sleep with it; live with it!

My question is simply this: "May I be allowed to be of service this day?" I make that prayer. Yes! Yes! Yes! Keep that question alive in your hearts, minds, and bodies, and you will be able to help. But do not complain if it is difficult. If every cell of our body resounds to the question, "May I be allowed to be of service this day?", then one day we will be allowed this. But if we do not ask, those cells will not resonate. We can presume in religion, presume in this, presume in that, but what is a question that every cell of your body can resound to? "Please, may I be allowed to be of service this day?"

To be able to be of service is a privilege. As our feet touch the ground in the morning, we ask in gratefulness, "May I be allowed to be of service?" It is a tremendous privilege. Much will happen from it, if you ask from gratefulness. If you ask with the wrong attitude, it will not be helpful for others or for yourself. If you ask correctly, it can help you and others.

The answer lies in the question. It always has and it always will. However, the question then arises: "What right do I have to ask the question?" Many times we have guilt, fear, resentment, envy and pride and we feel that perhaps we are not pure enough to ask a real question. But the human being is potentially perfect, and can manifest beauty.

How do we approach this question? We approach it quietly and tenderly, knowing that it is God's question. It is His question to us. "I give you everything. I give you life, I give you abilities, I give you the land, the sea, the air. In your world, I am Fire to burn away all the illusion that separates you from Me. Yet in another world I am the Grace through which you are transformed, and through your sacrifice I will be able to give you the ingredient needed to help a world that is waiting on the threshold of recovery."

P RAYER *"Prayer in unity can only come about through the realization of one's essential unity with God."*

If you pray, do not pray half-heartedly. Pray with every part of your being. Let your physical body resound to your intention, your feelings and your thoughts. Let prayer manifest in your life's motives and in your aspirational body. Beyond all else, trust that your prayers will be answered as they need to be answered.

Prayer is for the very brave. Self-pity, in the apparency of prayer, is for the very weak-hearted. Prayer carries the sound of intention, so let your prayer carry the sound of your deepest love, for most surely love is the cause of life and love is its own effect.

Understand that prayer is not limited to any religious belief system. It is universal as love is universal. Part of our life's work is to become so universal in our words, thoughts, feelings, and deeds that we become "the sounding box of God."

Jesus said, "I am thought being wholly thought." Energy is neutral. It is thought that makes it come into being. Look at the redemption of thought form. Can we see that the good will of the world is with us and gives us the strength to redeem thought form, the unredeemed negative thoughts? Positive thought is "Love the Lord thy God and love thy neighbor as thyself." We do not need any more than that. Love enters us, and in that, we do not have to do anything about the negative thought form, because it will go through us. We may have to wash a lot, though. The chalice is the symbol of emptiness. How many people have thought positively in the world? Many. We can say thank you. It all enters into the distillation, and eventually we have being. We do not accept negative thought form, because God asks us to follow only good. We have to be very humble to give up our negativity, to be able to receive good. If we can be empty for a moment of our stupidities and negativity, then all of the positive will enter us. It is up to us to give this good.

I am an instrument. "I am the flute, but the music is thine." What do we do with it? We should not do anything we do not want to do. We can be instrumental in any way we want. Then, something is happening. Give something every day. Each one of us has to find our own way of giving. It has to come from a living human being. In gratefulness, in remembrance, thousands will remember. It is said, "If we pronounce the Name of God correctly, immediately somebody is turning to God." It is said, "He is both the Name and the Named." And we are in the middle of it. If we are conscious, the wind may change to where it needs to go.

For inner understanding to take place, it is necessary for us to have rest. Let us call it "a still point in a turning world." You can receive this through another, but it can only be transmitted by somebody who knows. It is not what it appears to be. Each one of you, I pray, will take some rest every day. It does not take time to know. It already exists. Come into that point here in the heart, where distillation takes place, and every day make a moment of rest. If people come to us for help, it is only in that state of rest that we can really see, can truly hear. Truth lives in the heart, so take that rest. This comes through a transmission, even though in essence each of us already is complete. There is only one absolute Being.

Let us pray for each other and for the whole world. I certainly am humble enough to say that I also need help. I am sure that you need help. We all need help. Even God may need help.

To be humble enough to forgive is so difficult. Normality is a way to forgive. As normal human beings in the world, we can become instruments of the redemptive spirit of God, in forgiveness. He, which is beyond he or she, is both the Name and the Named. He is both the forgiver and the forgiven. He is *Hu Dost,* the Friend of all those who are brothers, who give their lives for eternity, who give their lives for the secret motive, let us say, of God. Remember that everything we see, everything we touch and everything we look upon is His Name. Remembering this, our children will be quite free. Everything is His Name. The pain of many people in the world is because we will not see His Name in one another.

Prayer in unity can only come about through the realization of one's essential unity with God. Prayer affirms the unity and brings the many into manifestation. It is possible to ask for specifics, but in the highest form of prayer we ask for nothing specifically, knowing that if we say "I will" in consciousness, we will be given exactly what we need to fulfill our part in the Divine Plan.

There is a whole hierarchy of "helpers" within the unity, existing on many planes of consciousness. Each one has a specific function, a job to do, so that the prayer that is made in love and consciousness can be answered. Each one of the helpers within the hierarchy of beings has control over those elements which are necessary, in whatever proportion, to bring about the answer to the prayer.

Beware! Once the elements have been invoked, and the command "Ride!" is given, they will go on to fulfill the command. It is necessary to get one's own personality and desires out of the way, for nothing can stand in the way of the great army of Light. Once they have been asked to help, they are then locked into the command. The riddle is that they are locked into the command until their own "death." Once they have fulfilled their job they are redeemed through man, through the very vehicle that made the request in the first place.

Knowledge is important. The acquisition of knowledge is vital if we are to be responsible human beings, able to fulfill what we have been asked to do, from the beginning of time, by our Lord. The greater the degree of knowledge, the more control we have, and the more possibility there is for the prayers to be answered. No more is there a haphazard answer to prayer. As we begin to understand the nature of prayer, life takes on a totally new meaning.

Above all, it is our attitude to prayer that is important. If we try to meditate for ourselves, or pray for ourselves, not knowing who or what we are, and not wanting to return to the one Source of all life, then we can fall into the danger of magic of one sort or another, landing disillusioned and miserable.

We come back, once again, to the three steps that are necessary: recognition, redemption, and resurrection. First we have to come to recognize the redemptive power of God. Then, in dying to all that we thought we were, as we rise on the planes in esoteric prayer, we are redeemed into worlds beyond our concepts of dimensions. We allow God to work through His hierarchy to bring perfect order into this world so that this world is changed. Finally, we come to know that indeed this world is the resurrection. The hereafter is here, now, after we realize it. This knowledge is only granted after we have died to all that we thought we were, all that, in our condition of sleep, we thought the world was.

Consciousness can be defined as "the reaction of active intelligence to pattern." To be able to pray we must be conscious. That means that we must be awake to who and what we are at any one moment. We cannot pray if we are asleep! We have to awaken our intelligence through will, through the Spirit, to be *active*. If we are conscious and if we are active, then true consciousness can come about. Active intelligence responds to the perfect pattern of the geometry of God so that the prayer can be answered. The invisible geometry which permeates all life begins to manifest itself through the planes, with much help. When we are actively engaged in prayer, we are turning to God, to our Lord, invoking all the help that is needed. God is one. There is only one Being. Within that unity, there is the miracle of His uniqueness. Each being, within Being, has its own job, its own unique job to do to help bring about the total redemption of man and of the planet itself.

Now we have some new ideas to look at. We can look at meditation techniques as being valid only to the extent that they enable us to give complete and undivided attention to the Beloved, who waits for that great moment when we can come to Him with all of our being. That is the great prayer, known in the West as, "Lord, have mercy on us." Mercy, His Mercy, bestows being. At the same time it takes away all that stands in the way of truth.

We can look at the many within the one that are needed to bring about the answer to prayer. We can contemplate further on the nature of geometry and what is often called the subtle anatomy of the body of God, all here, within, interpenetrating this space that we occupy. We can begin to look into the nature of intention and the right attitude to prayer, realizing our responsibility in being awake and being clean on all levels. We can understand that real consciousness can only come about when we are awake, when our intelligence, part of the overall Divine Intelligence, is awakened and, at last, active.

We can go still further and realize that mystical prayer, esoteric prayer, relates to the consciousness of higher "bodies." It is a state of levels or degrees of perception of reality. The "seven heavens" relate to consciousness, prayerful consciousness, in the various bodies. The mystical or spiritual marriage of the gnostics is the union of consciousness through the planes into oneness with the spiritual body.

DIE BEFORE YOU DIE *"To come into being we have to give everything up."*

When we die, and we are all going to die, we carry with us two things—preferably only one, but normally two. The first is everything that we think we need; and the second is the knowledge that we are at this very moment a unique aspect of God. If we know of the unity of God, there is no reincarnation—which is dependent only upon the needs we still think we have in this world. Thinking we need anything is an illusion.

And so we might ask, "Well what happens, then, when we die? Do we go on?" My reply is that we were here from the beginning of time. It is neither going on, nor going back, nor going up, nor going down. Death is the great illusion—death and conception are the same moment. All creation is in one moment and always has been in one moment.

Suppose we are going to die in life. We are going for the big one. That means dying every single moment of our lives. What we carry through death is anything we think we need and everything that we know we are. The latter is dependent on the lack or loss of the former. Every single moment we give up the idea that we need anything in this life brings us the possibility of having some knowledge of the truth of all life.

The French expression for orgasm is *le petit mort,* "the little death." If we could be like that, then we would be doing the work. We have no need, no need whatsoever. Work each day towards no need.

Lastly, I would like to say how to die. The answer is *giving.* The answer is in the word giving and nothing else, no thing else, no other word, no other expression. Only in giving totally will we have no need. That is the way to learn how to die, when we empty ourselves completely.

To come into being we have to give everything up. The world has one hand behind its back at the moment. If people on the spiritual path, including those people who have been in the work a while, have been given certain practices, they might be tempted to say, "Look what I've got!" Yet on the other hand they say, "I'm going to surrender." Maybe they switch hands. We always have something behind our backs that we cannot surrender, we cannot give up; so we cannot come into being. Could any of us actually give the whole lot up? There is no way of coming into the stage that we call "coming into being" without actually giving the whole lot up. This is very shocking sometimes.

We find that all the judgments we have made in our lives come back on us; we find that judgments from other people stick to us; we find that judgment has blocked our lives from the beginning of time. It has stopped the possibility of what I call the frightening freedom, the freedom that we cannot accept. We cannot realize the great freedom that is the freedom beyond every single thing that any of us know.

No system can take us to freedom, into being. It can lead us right to the edge. That is why we can say "Thank God" for all systems and ways. They are wonderful to lead us to the very point which we have to take off from. We have to take off and we have to make that great decision to say, "I will. I am prepared to die." As it is written in the *Koran*, "Die before you die."

I am a radical man. I dislike systems intensely, I dislike all form more than intensely. In any form, in any practice, we will not find freedom. Yet without such form, we will not reach that point where we can jump off. Say "Thank God" for all the things we have been given so far. Come right up to the edge of the swimming pool. Keep it light. Are we going to jump in or aren't we?

Free will, the free will to come into being, is what we know is so important in our lives together. It affords us the space to come into being.

When man says "I will" to his Lord, he will be given exactly what he needs to fulfill his part in the divine plan. Whatever he holds onto will only be taken away. Whatever a group holds onto will be taken away.

Coming into being is coming into gnosis, into knowledge. To come into that we leave everything behind. To understand what is behind what I am saying requires that we give up everything, every system, every practice, every thing we have ever learned. We come into our own being, which finally is His Being, not into anybody else's concept of what that might mean. Mevlana Jelaluddin Rumi, one of the great lovers of all time, said the following words: "Come, come, whoever you are—wanderer, worshipper, lover of leaving— it doesn't matter. Ours is not a caravan of despair. Come, even if you have broken your vow a thousand times. Come, come yet again, come." We come again and again, trying to come into being, trying to find our Lord, who will lead us into that state. But we carry with us a huge pack on our back. "Come, come yet again, come." Do not come with anything else. That does not mean to say we are disregarding the systems of the world, or the teachers of the world, or the churches of the world or any of those things. It is not that.

There is one God. There is one absolute Being. There is only one Teacher. There has only ever been one Messenger. Each moment manifests on Earth a certain attribute of God. He leads each one of us as we choose, towards the one goal which is the Lord. There is only one Teacher.

LORDSHIP *"We are creating through our attention, our love or lack of love, exactly what will be."*

It is possible to bow and kiss the feet of every teacher in the world, one after another. Each one is a manifestation of the Lord, of God. Not only is it possible, it is necessary. When we go to our Lord, we will manifest in the exterior world what we need to fulfill, what we have to do. Now we are possibly coming to understand the beginning of Lordship. St. Francis said, "What you are looking for is what is looking." Your Lord stands between one breath and another. Hazrat Inayat Khan once said, "Make God a reality and He will make you the truth." We could look at it this way: Make God a reality in your Lord, and you will understand. To come to understand Lordship, to come into being, we have to make the Lord a reality. How is this possible; how can we do this? How can we bring into being the impossible possibility, which is that our prayer may manifest on earth; that our turning to God, saying, "Thy Will be done, not mine," may manifest?

Maybe you can manifest balls of blue energy and do the whole flipping lot, but what comes out of it? Complete and absolute disenchantment. When we are brought to our knees, when we are on our death bed, even if we have done it all, even if we have been in country after country and have done this and done that, wanting to know the truth, what is it that comes to us? The longing for realization. What matters is the truth, and nothing but the truth. That is the point when we may understand coming into Being.

To come to that point we need incredible courage, because everything that we have ever learned has to be given up. We have to give up our education—that is our so-called education—all the stuffing down that was from without rather than that which was brought forth from within. We can give up and then we may come into the spiritual path, learning all sorts of interesting things and experiencing lovely effects. We may think we have found something. We may even think we are enlightened. That is the big one. But if we have ever been on our death bed, we will know that there is nothing we ever want but the truth. Everything else has to go. Everything. Every practice, everything. Then we turn to our Lord. We may say "Almighty God," we may say "Oh Lord," we may turn to our guru, or to our master, or whoever it may be. We turn at that moment and out of this may come the beginning of freedom. There are a thousand ways to that point, a thousand ways, but we end up at that point eventually.

Who is the Lord? What is Lordship? Our Lord may be Jesus Christ, the Virgin Mary, the physical manifestation of a teacher, or the understanding of the perfect teacher. Whatever it is, whatever name we choose, whatever aspect we choose, whatever concept we choose, it is still one thing. It is one great matrix, one blueprint, which will bring into birth our real self. "Make God a reality and He will make you the truth."

"Every single moment, every single moment of your life, you are your own forerunner," as Gibran once wrote. We are creating through our attention, our love or lack of love, exactly what will be. We are writing our own book. There is no guru outside us. There is no teacher outside us. There is nothing outside us. We are writing our own book. If we cannot face it inside ourselves, we will find it outside ourselves. It is the same thing. We will go on doing it until one day we are brought to our knees. And that is the beginning of freedom—it is the most joyous thing.

All the work that has been done, all the teachers that we have been given, everything is preparatory to the moment when one day we turn to our Lord, on our knees, literally or symbolically. At that point, there is nothing there. It is not only an emotional death, but even a spiritual death. That point comes to every human being, if we can face it.

T HE PATH OF THE MYSTIC *"Real faith is the invisible vehicle that will carry the mystic to his journey's end."*

The path of the mystic is an invisible path, traced out through the universe from the beginning of time. Its beginning, if there is any beginning, is set by the yearning of man to know his God, and its end, if there could ever be an end, is the knowing of God. It is a path of love, for only he who can truly love God can know Him. Only through the man who has come to love God perfectly can God's love be made completely manifest on Earth.

This invisible path, traced out step by step, following certain laws and patterns and moving into the center of the maze, is both the mystic's initiation into the Mysteries and his death before dying, his crucifixion and resurrection. His guides on the way are those who have already traveled that path and have returned to help others through the many pitfalls that beset the "madman" who wishes, above all things, to die to himself and be reborn in God.

There are two legs necessary for "walking the path." One leg represents the predestination in eternity of the divine possibilities latent in the heart of man, and the other is the leg of perseverance. One without the other is useless. The latent possibilities in the heart of man are hidden until they are brought out; perseverance is essential for this to occur. The movement of the two legs causes creative tension. Without creative tension there is no pruning, and without pruning, the veils that separate man from his own heritage of freedom and truth will not be lifted. Perseverance requires patience—one of the first qualities which needs to be developed in the mystic. He must have courage and strength. And he cannot afford to have a weak body, to be irresponsible about the vehicle that God gave him to realize himself in.

The mystic needs faith, faith almost like the blind faith of a little child praying to God. How can he come upon this faith? Few are born with real faith. Even those who begin the journey thinking they have faith are tried and tested so deeply that finally their faith is shaken to its very foundations. A new form of faith must then be built out of the ashes of the old. How does this faith come about, and how can it be developed in the heart of man? Real faith is the invisible counterpart of the physical vehicle that will carry the mystic to his journey's end.

Faith is developed from trust. I once thought that it was possible to develop a faith in the inevitable rightness of all life through a type of intellectual discipline that could be practiced every day. So I, like many others, worked on self-awareness, "waking up" exercises, and many hours of meditation. For a while this seemed to suffice. There was some sort of inner experience that led me to believe I was on the right path. I developed a sort of faith, it is true, but the faith was built on very unstable foundations. Where was the love element? Without love we are nothing, and we will understand nothing. Intellectual exercises and disciplines are useful to the mystic only in so far as they can awaken the intellect and keep the spirits high. Without the love of the heart, they mean NOTHING.

Because the foundations were unstable, there came a time when I realized that I had no faith at all. I only "thought" I had. Once again, like so many of us, I found it necessary to start all over. Then came the clue, which was like the key to opening the first door towards a real living faith in the one God. It is respect that opens the door to trust, and it is trust that is a prerequisite for the mystic's journey towards realization. To respect we must be aware. This is where the intellectual exercises that I had been taught came in useful for the first time. When we respect the God in someone, we begin to know the need of that human being. With awareness, we may be able to be instrumental in helping them unfold what is waiting to be brought forth from the Light.

And what a delight this is! A whole new invisible world is opened up to us. The inner world, which *is* a world of Light, is seen in the joy of another. It is the beginning of the realization of stillness.

This is the very beginning of the journey of the mystic into the unknown. All that has happened before, the disciplines and the practices, are preparation for the breaking open of the first veil, the first degree of realization as the mystic approaches his Lord. Suddenly, almost unexpectedly, the light of the soul is seen to shine through another. Yet, there is just the faintest intuition that it is not so much that *person's* light, but rather a Light that was always there, wishing to be recognized and seen in the world. At times like this a person may become completely transfigured, and a joy can spring forth. The light that breaks out into the open will enable that person to see the same light in others. There can be the beginning of true communication, the chance of a mystical embrace, and perhaps the early beginnings of the mystical dialogue that takes place between God and man.

The real journey has begun! At this stage, it may seem almost easy. We might wonder why there is so much written about the path, for surely here it all is in front of us. By being open to His Light shining through us we become instrumental in lighting another, and thus there is joy. We can see His Light shining through the other, and perhaps for a moment we can know what it is like to be able to bow to the God in man, to see the "withinness of things," and to experience the essence without the form. In fact, the forms just collapse around us in the realization of Light.

In the path of the mystic, no matter what his label (i.e., Christian, Moslem, Jewish, etc.), there are various stages along the journey which are the different stages of realization. Each one brings forth a greater rapture in the heart as forms dissolve in the realization of the Essence. To explain these stages, we need some sort of language. It is in the language of the Sufis, and particularly of Ibn al Arabi, that I would like to explain two of these stages, which we call *fana*. *Fana* is the passing away of all illusion, and in its place there comes what we call *baqa,* which is the endurance of the Real. To every stage of *fana* must come a stage of *baqa*. Here is a warning for us all. The path of the mystic is a knife-edged path. It is long, and in a sense it is dangerous, for in the mystic's desire to die before death, he might pass into a stage of *fana* which Arabi calls "imperfect." He might realize for an instant that in his limited ego-consciousness he has no existence *per se*. Yet God gave him a form through which realization could occur. If the mystic loses consciousness at this point, he goes into a state which is described as "sleep." He is neither with his self nor is he with his Lord.

In the final stage, the mystic in his rapturous flight contemplates God as the Essence of the universe rather than the Cause of it. He can no more say that the universe is the effect of a cause, but rather is a "reality in appearance." He realizes the meaninglessness of causality. This is the ultimate goal of the mystic, for he sees the two worlds as one. He knows that in reality immanence and transcendence are one. This is the fixing of gold in alchemy, the sun in the heart. The ego has been transformed and the essence takes over. Yet the goal is not God. How can it be God, when He is the very one that "arrived" at the goal? Now the sentence, "I was a hidden treasure and I longed to be known," is realized, and the secret of all creation is understood. The supreme happiness of the mystic is realized, for he KNOWS of his essential unity with

God, and at this moment of divine wonder, God contemplates Himself perfectly. Only in the perfect man, who is able (through his mystical station) to love God perfectly, can the treasure, which is the hidden essence, be made manifest on Earth.

THE SYMBOLISM OF THE WEDDING CEREMONY *"When true freedom is attained, we must return to the world to bring it new life."*

The symbolic meaning and purpose of marriage was once understood, but today it is not difficult to see that it has been forgotten. Originally marriages were "arranged." The bride and bridegroom seldom saw one another beforehand. The boy had to achieve manhood before a bride was found for him. He had to be a man, and that meant that he, in the image of prayer, had to be brave, courageous and forbearing. He had to be awake, ready to go to battle to defend his heritage at any moment. He had to develop will, so that he had no fear of death and was always ready to do whatever was asked of him.

After he attained his manhood, the leaders would set about finding a suitable bride for him. At the same time, a woman was being prepared by her mother and the women of the tribe or particular family. Through this preparation she gained knowledge of womanhood and the role she had to play in the unfolding of the Divine Will. She learned how woman is all space, knowing everything at once, whereas man knows only one thing at a time. She realized why man and woman need each other to bring about alchemical fusion in the perfect marriage. Eventually, the wise men, using certain methods from the esoteric sciences, would choose the bride. Although it is easy to look at the world of form, this was actually a marriage arranged in Heaven, the wise men being merely representatives of the wisdom of God.

I will use the symbolism of the Christian Church to illustrate the inner meaning of the marriage of man and woman. After the bride had been found, the future bridegroom would turn to the woman and say, "Will you marry me?" She, in order to bring about the first stage of the ceremony, would say, "I will." We will note here how the word "will" is used. Once he had asked the question and she had agreed, preparations would be made for the ceremony itself. Clothes were made for the bride, the dowry was discussed, a house was prepared for the couple and, obviously, much activity and energy was directed towards the great day of the ceremony. On that day the guests, coming to witness the promises made by the couple in front of the priest, would assemble in the church, divided on either side; one side being the guests and family of the bride and the other, the guests and family of the bridegroom. The aisle up the middle can be seen to be the straight way toward union.

The bridegroom arrives first with his best man. The job of the best man is merely to get the bridegroom to the church on time, "properly dressed," and to bring the rings that are to be exchanged. Here, of course, physical clothes are only the manifestation of the invisible garments that are necessary— the different "bodies" that need to be developed, pure and ready to receive the Spirit. The night before the wedding the men all go out together to drink wine and toast the future bridegroom. Wine is the symbol of the Spirit in the ceremony. The bridegroom, having come into manhood and having developed will, is asked to be infused with the Spirit of God in order to fulfill his job as a man and as a husband.

The bridegroom waits at the front by the low altar rails and an air of expectancy permeates the church. At that time, no one really knows whether the bride is going to arrive at all. As is well known, she seldom arrives on time! Quiet music is playing throughout the church and then, as the bride enters, escorted by her father who is to give her away, the wedding march is played. Coming into the church veiled, the bride walks up the aisle towards her future husband. The priest turns to greet them, everyone stands, and the ceremony commences. When the bride reaches the altar rail, the bridegroom steps towards her. The father steps back, having completed his job. The best man, once he has given the rings, has also completed his particular task. During the wedding ceremony itself, the priest asks certain promises of the couple. The reply to these questions is both "I will" and "I do." Here again, I ask that we look into the inner meaning of these words, for it is true that without will we cannot "do" anything! At a certain time the veil is lifted and, after the ceremony is complete and the rings are exchanged, the couple then kiss. This kiss is surely the manifestation of God's blessing.

Still, the congregation has not seen the face of the bride. The priest leads the couple to the high altar where he addresses them in private. When he has said what has to be said, the couple turns around, facing the congregation, and the organ bursts into the music of glorification. The couple walk back down the aisle, representing the way of truth, love, compassion and service, out of the church and back into the world.

Think of the wonder and glory of such a ceremony. Rather than interpret all the inner meanings, let me leave a few keys, so that the "hidden treasure" may be revealed. The bride comes dressed in white, and with a long train behind her. The train is upheld, dependent upon the "station" of the couple, by a certain number of pages and bridesmaids. In a royal family, these may be up to eight in number. The "train" represents the whole invisible world, longing to return to the one Source of all life, which can only come about through the alchemical fusion of man and woman. The One divides in order to unite back into the One. The low altar rail where the couple are married represents the dividing line between the lower nature of man and to the soul itself. The high altar represents the Ocean from which all comes and to which all returns. It is said that a Sufi is "a drop that becomes the Ocean." The drop here is the fusion of these two elements of male and female. The words, spoken in secret by the priest at the high altar, open the gateway to true freedom. When true freedom is attained, we must return to the world to bring it new life; and so the couple turn back and walk down the way that they have traversed. It is then that their lives begin as a true act of service in His Name. They have given up their wills to the greater Will, and can now bring His Will to a waiting world.

THE LIMITATIONS OF THE MIND *"The Divine Guidance is to bring us to the point of perplexity."*

Throughout history, teachers have attempted to pass on an inner knowledge which is virtually impossible to transmit directly, since the mind is always attempting to understand by comparing one thing to another. Because of the nature of the mind, various ways have been devised to transmit this knowledge. One of these is the telling of stories or parables.

Let us look at the mind for a moment. The support of the mind is based entirely upon comparison. For the mind to be still and thus for real understanding to come about, this grinding clash of opposites that exists within the mind must be eradicated.

First of all, the mind assumes that it can know, not realizing that it is an instrument of will, of the spirit. All it can actually do is produce greater and greater comparisons since, if we consider it, the mind is based upon words and words always have a relative opposite. For instance, when we say, "This tree has green leaves," somewhere or other the mind is attempting to come to grips with comparing green with another color. Or we may say, within the mind, "This is spring," and automatically there is a picture somewhere within the subconscious of summer, winter, or fall.

As I said before, the support of the mind is based entirely upon comparison, and that implies that there is more than one. Yet in reality there is only One! To be free means that we come to know, through direct perception of the truth, that there is only One and, at the same time, that the One divides into many.

The mind needs to learn to see from the perspective of the One and the many at the same time. The mind thrives on sequential thinking, meaning that first there is "this" and then there is "that." The mind feels happy with this as it continues to move along the sequential line. If we are to truly understand, we have to come to realize that there is another faculty within man and woman which can directly perceive the truth and come to realize that time and eternity are one. Al-Hallaj once said, "Time is the eternal attribute of God." That statement was not made by the mind of Al-Hallaj, but was spoken in words from the realization that indeed all creation is in one moment. "The moment of creation contains everything in latency within itself." In that one moment, space is made for continually renewed creation in time.

Ibn al Arabi once said, "The Divine Guidance is to bring us to the point of perplexity." Here, of course, he was referring to that inner guidance which, through will, correct motive, and intention in ourselves, can bring the mind to such a point of perplexity that it realizes that it does not know. Stories can bring us to the point of perplexity as long as we want to know the truth. If all we want is an explanation of the truth, then the stories or parables that we are given to study mean very little. Each real story contains within it the "hidden secret." "I was a hidden treasure and I longed to be known, so I created the world that I might be known." The "hidden treasure" lies within these stories, for the stories are written from essence. They are both eternal and temporary ("of time") in the relative world. Thus, even if we were to read one of these stories a hundred times, there would always be a new and inner meaning manifested through it.

What the mind cannot understand is that everything is in one moment. Yet here, in this world, everything is seen in change. God has never manifested Himself twice in the one moment in the relative sense, for that could not be.

Let us look further into this. Mevlana teaches us to "look to the signs." What we see in the relative world are signs of the manifestation of Divine Law. If we see only what appears to be in the relative world, we are missing the point. If I look out of my window and see the mountains, the sun, and the wind moving the branches of the pine trees, and I become identified with this, I fail to understand just why all this has been given to me. I assume, or I take it for granted, that what I see is reality, rather than understanding that what I see is the appearance of reality.

When He said, "I was a hidden treasure and I longed to be known," He was and is telling us that He creates this apparency through which we can come to know Him. This world is like a shadow, but the shadow is inevitably attached to that which projects it. We must remember that it is light—the all-apprehending light of God—that allows the shadow to exist in the first place. If there were no light, then there would be no shadow. At the same time, there is something which stands between the light and the shadow.

What I have just said is difficult to put into words. One way I might try to transmit this knowledge would be to write a book of stories attempting to awaken that inner faculty of man which is so often veiled by the limitations of the mind.

We are attempting to break beyond the limitations of the mind and even beyond consciousness itself. Do we not wish for this freedom? Is what appears to be, in the relative world, enough? Can we start to make the sacrifices necessary to come upon that eternal truth (which is, and has always been, at once)?

It is said, "A Sufi is one who sees God in creation, and creation in God, at the same moment." A real Sufi is able to see the divine principle. There is only one eternal moment in which all life exists, existed, and will exist for evermore.

The word "recognition" comes from the word "gnosis," and that means, as I said before, direct perception of the truth itself. Recognition means finding the eternal knowledge that lies within the soul. The soul is a substance, a very fine substance, that is impossible to describe and which, paradoxically enough, grows into knowledge through surrender and sacrifice.

THE CREATION OF A SOUL
"The soul is a knowing substance."

Until we can consciously be in the present moment, the very idea of "doing" anything can be seen to be nothing more than mere fantasy. It has also been said that although we have something called a "soul," it is only in its embryonic state. All of the mystery schools have stressed that we need to gain this immortal soul through continuous work on ourselves. Until this is achieved, we will continue to live in a world of sequential time with one event appearing to follow another and one problem manifesting another problem. It is not difficult to realize that such a life within sequential time is a life of continuous suffering that is mainly unconscious.

Essentially, a school is set up to fulfill a particular function in the realization that, since everything in life is interconnected, we can really do nothing alone. Thus, when a group of people meet consciously as an act of service, certain possibilities are opened up. If we attend a school it is presumably because we want to learn and also because we have realized that we do not yet know what we wish to know or what we need to know.

The soul can only be developed by a long process of accumulating and crystallizing the finest energy which the physical and psychic organism can produce, through a continuous attempt to become awake. Ordinary man cannot help spending his energy, as fast is it is produced, on fear, anger, envy, longing, or his normal state of fascination with himself and the world around him. In order to restrain this wasting of energy, he must create will in himself. In order to create will, he must have one aim. In order to have one aim, he must learn all sides of himself, and help them to accept the domination of his conscience. He needs to awaken his conscience from sleep and realize that none of these stages can be achieved by himself alone.

The creation of a soul during our physical lifetime is the greatest task that we can possibly attempt. The question might arise as to whether this is a selfish act. In fact, it is not selfish, for we have realized, through our work, the latent gift which rightfully belongs to God and which can be returned to its Source.

Every single cell in the body has memory and also what we might call consciousness. I can make an analysis of somebody's condition to help them not to repeat the habit patterns that have made them so unhappy. I can go through the different cells, the physical and etheric counterparts in five dimensions, discovering what has happened during this lifetime to block time or crystallize a moment of time—i.e., shock. First of all, we see experiences of pain in people as negative. But these experiences are neither negative nor positive, for often they are what bring us to the point of yearning for truth. The pain is merely a visiting card to call us to acknowledge a reality beyond our personal experience.

There is in most cases a memory pattern in the cells that is always related to our concept of ourselves. The apparency of oneself is an illusion, since in reality we do not exist as separate from the divine reality. What are we actually remembering in those crystallized moments of time? We are merely recollecting the shock and pain of particular events that have occurred in our lives. Fear, grief, and self-pity, for example—which certainly are not attributes of God—were coupled with a situation which probably helped to crystallize that moment. Agreement to the crystallization of the moment of shock becomes a limitation to the soul. This is a limitation to the ecstatic flight of the mystic, which is freedom. The agreement can result from physical shock. In reality there is always something which has crystallized the shock. If one is out in the woods and cuts one's finger off, the shock will remain as a memory. The moment the shock waves come back from the environment or experience, crystallization of that moment takes place in memory.

There is a memory pattern in the cells which we make through our false ego. If the soul is a knowing substance, meaning it knows everything at once and one thing at a time, it can open Pandora's box. That is, it can know the "secret book" or the "hidden treasure." The substance of the soul comes from sacrifice; through sacrifice comes redemption, or at least the possibility of redemption.

The soul is formed through sacrifice and surrender. It cannot be acquired. Knowledge is given and not acquired. Being is bestowed through our sacrifice.

Imagine a mortar into which we put all the sacrifice. Somebody then comes in with a big pestle and keeps grinding it. What appears to be your sacrifice and my sacrifice suddenly is seen to be just sacrifice. No longer is it yours or mine because in reality there is no longer you or me. Down here, it is necessary for there to be a you and me, but in reality we are not divided. Into this beautiful mortar someone then adds a little moisture, and then the paste is made. The paste relates to eternal time. The transformation of subtle energies occurs within a crystallized moment. Each degree of sacrifice, by individuals, by a group, and by society, leads us further into the development of the soul.

There is a seat for the Christ within us. There is a seat for every master, saint and prophet within us. If we go on making sacrifice, we realize that we do not have sixteen guides at once. There is only one Teacher, one Guide. The further we go, the more mortar contains everything, until at last there is only He. A knowing soul is part of the substance of everything; it is not separate, yet it is separate. This soul is not separate. You have your inner possibility and I have mine; yet still there is only one possibility. They are all sparks of the universal soul.

Let us briefly sum up what the substance is and how it relates to time. The substance of the soul is made of the "stuff" that comes through sacrifice and surrender. It is the redemption of false time. If we could surrender with every breath, we could really be here. What can begin to be here is the substance.

"Let your bread be baked with burning tears," and "Be washed with the blood of the heart." It starts off with a great yearning, "O my God," then it goes further, becoming, "O Thou," and finally, "O I." One person has built his or her soul body, which is divisible into as many persons as one trusts. To make gold in alchemy we first need gold.

THE ALCHEMY OF THE HEART *"It is through recognition that the Beloved is freed."*

It is said that a Sufi is "a drop that becomes the Ocean." It is also said, in most esoteric traditions, that it is necessary to gain one's immortal soul in order to come into realization. So it is important to consider the nature of the soul that we have to gain and to understand the drop that becomes the ocean.

We start our journey into the unknown having really no idea what it is we are looking for. We know that it is because of pain, or a sense of rejection in one situation or another, that we go off in search of the elusive something that will relieve us of our pain and bring us to true freedom.

We may find that we are poorly equipped for the journey. We go through a period, sometimes of many years, during which we do work on ourselves through meditation, through yoga, through movement, or through this practice or that. These practices have two effects. First, they help prepare the vehicle to work with the energies that manifest themselves as we proceed along the path; and second, these practices contain a hidden trap.

The trap is that it is so easy to forget what we originally set out to find. We get so keen on working on ourselves that we even choose to put the quest out of our minds, since as soon as we consider it once again, there arises once more the very pain, the yearning, that set us off on our journey. Yet, without that yearning, which is sometimes called conscious suffering, it is not possible to come upon the object of our search.

There are many legends in history connected with this search. We have only to look at one or two to be reminded that this search has gone on from the beginning of time. Think, for instance, of the tales of the Princess trapped in the castle, doomed to remain there for the rest of her life until the Prince comes and frees her through his love.

In one of these legends, the Prince is walking in a deserted city when he feels something stick to the sole of his shoe. When he bends down, he finds a small gold key that can unlock the castle gates. The gold key is this world, which is ultimately recognized to be the resurrection itself.

In these legends, it is the love of the Prince that unites him with his Princess. On the journey to find her, he has to undergo all sorts of tests and privations to prove that he is worthy to finally come to her. He must develop certain qualities, such as courage, will, patience, and compassion. At each stage these tests lead him to the very brink of disaster, but because of the intensity of his yearning for the beloved he gets through. Always he is helped by someone who appears out of nowhere to lead him back onto the path from which he has strayed.

The key to understanding these legends is contained in two words, "love" and "recognition." It is through love and because of love that we search for the Beloved. It is through recognition that the Beloved is freed and we discover, finally, that we ourselves are love, lover, and beloved. We are the Prince who searches, the Princess who is finally set free through recognition, and we are the very impetus itself that set us out on our searching.

The idea that the soul is a knowing substance brings a further dimension into play: knowledge. It is knowledge that leads us to love, and without knowledge, love, which is pure energy, cannot be anchored and fixed.

Love without knowledge is virtually useless; hence the tremendous stress on study. There is always a great danger that study may be misinterpreted and get us caught in a cerebral concept about the object of our search. Once again, we could forget what it is that started us on this journey. Then the yearning would come no longer from the heart, but from a part of us that longs for more and more knowledge. We may unconsciously discover that with sufficient study the pain is lessened and even forgotten in the many concepts of the One. We could become trapped in a series of new veils, and yet the Princess is still crying from her window, waiting to be released into that terrific freedom.

Knowledge must be balanced with love, that is, balanced by the yearning of the heart for the Beloved. Love is the cause of all creation and wants only to be recognized. It is love itself that finally strips away all the veils so that it can be seen in the pure light of realization.

Knowledge and power are one. That is why it is so important that in putting ourselves in the stream of service we always make our own will subsidiary to the greater will, the Will of God. As we start to be given knowledge (knowledge is given and not acquired), we are also given power, which must be returned to the Source of all life. As we say in the Lord's Prayer, "For Thine is the Kingdom, and the Power, and the Glory."

If we forget that we are nothing, that there is only one absolute Being, then we spiritualize the ego and not the heart. We then become possessed by power itself, craving more and more food for the ego.

If we are continuously giving and if we remain in the path of service, our food becomes the Spirit, and everything we need is provided for us. It may not be what we think we want, for we cannot know what we really need. It is thought that divides us from the truth itself. It is only thought that can create concepts of oneness, bringing about division and separation.

Let us return to the word "soul." We might also call it "the essential self." Whatever we term it, there is the essential part of our nature, which must be found before we can know what the real object of our search was in the first place. In one of the traditions, it is only when man reaches the number nine, that of perfected man, that he is termed the seeker, or "the seeker after truth."

Imagine a high mountain, with a great light bursting from its summit. A path winds up the mountain. Standing at the bottom is a man whose heart is shining with the same light as that at the mountain top. He gazes for the first time at the peak of the mountain, having traveled across the world to become perfected, to come to love as perfectly as a man can. His love of God has become first in his life, outstripping all other loves, all other dreams, all other aims.

God fulfills His promise to man by taking away all the veils so that the seeker, the mystic, may see Him face to face in the pure light of the soul, the light of pure intelligence.

The soul is a knowing substance. The soul is made of the stuff, or substance, of redeemed energy—energy that has returned to the Source of all energy through man, through the alchemy of the heart. It is not a very romantic notion to be told that what we are is a vehicle for the transformation of subtle energies, but this is exactly what we are.

If we turn to our Lord, then we may find that our prayer can be of service. There is nothing else that we could want than to be of service to the Beloved, the object of our search.

This substance to which we refer cannot be understood with the discursive mind, but it can be understood through the direct perception that comes with the awakening of the heart. Clues can be given as to its nature, but that is all.

It is said that Christ, or Spirit, is the redeemer of the world. He comes to redeem us that we may come into freedom, which is the true heritage of the soul itself. Through Christ, the heart (which is the seat of the soul) takes wing and man takes his proper place, standing on the crescent moon within the heart itself. The heart becomes the only place big enough to reveal the essence of God. "There is nowhere big enough to contain Me, but the heart of My faithful servant contains Me."

The alchemy of the heart is the total transformation that is necessary within man for gnosis, knowledge of God, to occur. Man has to turn himself inside out, as it were, and come to realize, as a living reality and not just as an intellectual concept, that there is nothing outside of himself. Within his armspan there are limitless universes.

Whenever man truly surrenders, turns totally to his Lord, a universe is born. And whenever man finds himself, a whole galactic system bursts into life.

In alchemy there is the saying, "As above, so below." Although complete transformation takes time in the world, in reality transformation is instantaneous, since all creation is in one moment of time. "As above, so below" means that the two worlds are instantaneously seen to be one when we realize our essential unity with God. Christ, redeeming the world, brings this world of illusion into the real world, transforming the false into the real. Finally, we come to understand that this world is the resurrection, and that both immanence and transcendence are one. *Haqq* (the Real) and *Khalq* (Appearance) are one and identical. The One and the many, time and eternity, all are One.

This process is instantaneous in the real world and continuous in this world. The untransformed mind cannot understand the nature of the soul. Mind must be redeemed, so that we can be given the direct insight which provides us with the knowledge we need, and which frees us at the same time.

A key can be given here, which may unlock the door of the heart if we have truly entered the path of service. Christ, or Spirit, comes to redeem the world, to redeem those aspects of one pure energy, so that everything is returned to the Source, so that the drop once again becomes the Ocean from which it came.

Yet what is Spirit? Spirit is redeemed energy. "As above, so below." Spirit is both that which redeems, and that which is redeemed through and within man.

Only when we put ourselves in the path of service can this be understood; for as we give, so we receive. Once we take this great plunge into the unknown, giving away continuously all that we are given, we are filled with the Spirit of God which is waiting to redeem us. This can only come about through the sacrifice of all that we think we are.

The three stages of recognition, redemption, and resurrection take place in less time than the opening and closing of an eye. Then we may discover the essential self, the soul, which is made of the very substance of redeemed energy and which is that which redeems. Thus the Christ is found within, the alchemical marriage has taken place, and the real seeker is born.